JO: The 4-5-6

From: Brianna,
On her Birthday

2/23/99

SHADOW WALKERS

SHADOW WALKERS

RUSS CHENOWETH

CHARLES SCRIBNER'S SONS • NEW YORK
Maxwell Macmillan Canada • Toronto
Maxwell Macmillan International
New York • Oxford • Singapore • Sydney

Charles Scribner's Sons Books for Young Readers
Macmillan Publishing Company
866 Third Avenue, New York, NY 10022

Maxwell Macmillan Canada, Inc.
1200 Eglinton Avenue East, Suite 200
Don Mills, Ontario M3C 3N1

Macmillan Publishing Company is part of
the Maxwell Communication Group of Companies.
First edition   10 9 8 7 6 5 4 3 2 1
Printed in the United States of America

Library of Congress Cataloging-in-Publication Data
Chenoweth, Russ.
Shadow walkers / Russ Chenoweth. — 1st ed.   p.   cm.
Summary: Three inquiring young rats set out from their highly
civilized community on a journey across Cape Cod to explore
their surroundings and learn more about humans and the world.
ISBN 0-684-19447-3
[1. Rats—Fiction. 2. Cape Cod (Mass.)—Fiction.]   I. Title.
PZ7.C4196Sh 1993   [Fic]—dc20   92-18798

For John, the first reader,
and in memory of my father, the first storyteller

· 1 ·

It was very quiet in the woods. This was one of the oldest hardwood groves on the Cape, a remnant of the great forest that had once covered the entire peninsula from the ocean to the bay. Although the trees topped the hill above her den, Sara had been here only a few times in her life, and never before alone.

The woods weren't particularly dangerous for rats, but there was little of interest to them here. There was nothing much to eat—that was the reason, really. Sara smiled to herself. That was what it often came down to with water rats.

She listened, hardly breathing. The sounds of traffic on the mid-Cape highway were faint and distant. Nothing moved on the forest floor. There were few signs of life up here compared with the teeming fields and marsh below. No, that was silly. There were fewer living things, perhaps, but the great creature in front of her was monstrously alive.

1

The grandfather oak was the tallest tree on the hill, and it was the one she had come to climb.

Rats are good climbers, but rats are good at many things that they are ordinarily too sensible to do. If Sara had told her parents what she planned, they would have asked her not to do it because it was dangerous and unnecessary. So she hadn't told them, and that troubled her. Her parents were kind and reasonable. She loved and respected them, and usually she obeyed and tried to please them. This time she had made her own decision. She had climbed other trees, and she was strong and sure and not afraid. The danger was slight, she felt, and it was something she had to do.

The trunk rose above her like a wall for thirty feet before the first great limb jutted out, as large itself as a good-sized tree. Beyond that the branches grew thickly, and the trunk began to taper toward the light and shadow of the leafy canopy. Sara climbed, carefully and surely, stopping every few feet to listen. She was exposed here and nearly defenseless, but still nothing moved in the woods. She felt safer when she had reached the limb and could stretch out for a moment on the rough bark and look and listen. Five minutes of careful climbing brought her to the highest branch. It was no more than two inches in diameter at its base and reached straight up, above all the branches of all the other trees in the woods. This had been her goal.

Two feet below the highest leaf, she had to stop. The branch had shrunk to less than half an inch and bowed slightly with her weight. It was high enough. Above her the early-morning sky was clear and blue. A soft cool breeze brought the smell of the sea, and below her the

Cape was spread out in a vast crescent. Trees and sky merged in distant blue shadows to the south, and to the north the bay beach curved thirty miles, to the dunes beyond Cape End. North Cape and the dunes—that was a place she'd really like to go.

She'd seen satellite photos of the Cape and even bits and pieces of this scene from other vantage points, but for the first time in her life she saw it as a whole, her Cape, serene and lovely in the morning sun. Her field and den were hidden by the trees, but she could see the marsh to the east and the old Coast Guard station and the lighthouse beyond. The steeple of Saint Paul's soared above the trees directly to the north of her, and to the west a line of fishing boats headed out into the bay from Stone Harbor. Gulls sailed purposefully from bay to sea, and two hawks circled very high above. Up here the gentle sea wind drove all the usual distant summer sounds away, the trucks and diggers, hammers, drills, and power saws. Except for a water tower and a few slim antennas, there was no sign of the many roads and houses and other artifacts of human culture that dotted the Cape beneath the thickly growing pitch-pine forest. It looked as it might have looked to the Pilgrims nearly four centuries ago and to the Nauset Indians for a thousand years before that. And at the moment it was hers.

She spent ten minutes on her branch, breathing in the pungent air and looking out across the gray-green land and blue-green sea that lay beneath a pale morning sky. This was her world, every place she had ever been spread out before her like a map. It was exactly what she had hoped to see, and yet she had a sense of disappointment. It all was there, as familiar to her as a chessboard, but no helpful text supplied the rules. Nothing was explained, not who she was or what she was to do. Was that what she had hoped to find up here? She felt the warmth of the sun on her back and saw the branches and leaves around her glow in a burst of morning light. It all appeared quite ordinary close at hand, exactly like the three-foot scrub oaks that edged the field a hundred feet below.

She never knew what made her glance down in time to see the shadow glide among the dim trunks with the silence of a moth and settle on a limb below her. It was an owl, a very big one, and he had decided for some idiotic reason to change his daytime perch and come to join her in her tree.

She wasn't afraid at first. The unlikely lunacy of the thing was almost comical. But he was there, and she was swaying in the breeze no more than fifty feet above him, and here she'd stay until the owl left on his evening hunt or she grew weak or dizzy and fell to become his unexpected meal.

He couldn't see her against the light—he or she. It didn't matter—she'd get no concession either way. Owls had little sense of smell, but they could hear a seed drop on the forest floor. She'd better not shake off any acorns. He would hear her move or cough. He might even hear her breathing if the wind fell off. This wouldn't do. She didn't know if he could take her up here in the leaves and sunlight, but she'd never last till dark. Dark was his element, anyway. He might wait all day, knowing she was there, and then in darkness come and pick her off the branch like a ripened peach. She'd never get past him, though, not down in the twilight of the great tree trunks. She fumed in anger

4

and frustration. She was surprised that she felt no fear. Maybe it was because there was only one way down and no decision to be made. Just the one almost surely fatal course. At least no one would know about her foolishness. She'd simply disappear. That was the usual way with rats, until they got too old to go on the land at all. No one would ever know what had happened to her, and they'd all be very sad.

She was just about to shed her own tears at her family's sorrow when an acorn fell from a branch below her and struck the limb above the owl. Not a feather flickered. The sound had startled her, however, and for the first time she felt afraid. He must have heard it hit. It had echoed like a gunshot in the silent forest. She heard another fall in a nearby tree, and then a third. There were acorns dropping all around her. She'd heard them all along, she realized. What was more natural in a stand of oaks? They'd mean nothing to the owl. Could it even help her? Could her scramble down the tree be hidden by the sounds of falling acorns? It seemed unlikely. Another fell from the branch below her, and this one struck the owl's own limb. The owl flinched. Sara considered the bird a moment. He looked a great deal like a big stuffed specimen sitting worn and dusty on its perch. Slowly and carefully she reached out and twisted an acorn from a twig. She thought a moment about the distance and the trajectory and then threw it at the owl. It sailed behind his head like a bullet. All wrong! Not even owls were that simple, but he hadn't moved. Could she toss another now? How long normally would a tree wait between acorns? How idiotic—acorns fell when they were ready. Well, they were ready in this tree. She

5

tossed the next one in a gentle curve, and it plunked directly onto the owl's round head. He twitched again, in quiet rage, presumably. It took another seven acorns and three more hits before old Newton got the message that this was an unusually productive tree. Without a sound he launched himself into the air and swiftly disappeared among the somber trunks.

Sara waited for a few more minutes, to be sure the owl wasn't planning to return and that even the memory of his annoyance with the oak would have seeped from his tiny brain. Then she carefully climbed down.

She rested briefly on the leaf mold of the forest floor, until her breathing had slowed and the trembling in her limbs had calmed, and then she headed for the sunlit field. She didn't stop until she felt the comfortable cool stone of her own front entrance beneath her paws.

Sara stood there for a moment and looked out across the green and pleasant marsh below, feeling both excitement and relief. She had done it, and it had been far more of an adventure than she had planned. The owl had posed an unexpected danger, but she'd gotten around him by her wits. She wished she could tell her brother Peter. He might think her foolish, though, to have gotten into such a scrape at all. What had the experience taught her? That she was smart enough and not a coward? Not the sort of thing you had to prove. It hadn't told her what to do. How could it?

The view, of course, had been as splendid as she'd hoped, a sight not many rats had seen. She wished she had the words and skill to share with her friends the sweep of sea and sky, the familiar woods and far horizon. Well, she'd not forget this morning ever, and she wouldn't have to climb the tree again. Though now . . . She almost laughed, for what she'd done, she realized, was set herself another evidently pointless goal, a journey to the distant dunes beyond Cape End, much farther than a treetop on her hill.

The smell of breakfast wafted from the entrance to the den. She shook away the faintest chill and went inside.

·2·

Peter watched from an opening in the tall grass as the large tiger cat progressed down the back steps of the library building and stood at the top of the path, only its whiskers showing any interest in the scene below. A few determined stars pierced the mist to spread a faint light on the hill and the dark pond at its foot. The usual shrill chorus of cicadas filled the summer night with song.

"Melvil," Peter called softly.

"Peter? I thought I smelled a rat."

Peter laughed politely and came up the path to where the big cat waited.

"It's good to see you, Peter. Will you come in for coffee?"

"Thank you, I'd like that." The pleasure in the old animal's voice had startled him. He hadn't realized that his visits were important to the library cat. He followed Melvil up the stairs and through the flap into the workroom and then down the dark corridor to the kitchenette. Miss Lang, the librarian, had had her last cup of tea an hour earlier and turned the library over to Melvil, as she'd say, though perhaps more thoroughly than she intended.

"Is this a social visit, Peter, or would you like to use the collection?"

"A bit of both," Peter answered with a twinge of guilt. "I did mean for us to have a talk."

"Well then," said the cat, "it had best be over coffee." He flipped on the light and bustled about the pots and pans while they talked of the small doings of the mid-Cape. They had much to tell one another. Melvil shared in all the gossip that went on between Miss Lang and her corps of volunteers and a stream of chatty patrons. Few creatures knew more about the Cape than he, but he accepted cat food from a can and rarely strayed beyond library property except to visit relatives. Peter, on the other hand, knew every rock and hole between the ocean and the bay and had a nodding acquaintance with half the skunks and badgers and all the rats for miles around. He had a more fleeting familiarity with the fox and some knowledge of the local hounds.

His friendship with Melvil was unique. Most cats kept to themselves or confined their sociability to other cats. The local wildlife spurned them all, of course, as compromised by domesticity, referring to them scornfully as household pests, along with dogs and parakeets.

The rats, by contrast, were admired and feared, though equally avoided. The fear was unjustified, but fully understandable. Most animals made do. Rats had made their own society. Its outlines were flexible but strong, and their culture was very old and deep. Peter's own species, the Norway rat, was the largest and most widespread, and they were familiar to their human neighbors by many names: the house rat, the sewer or wharf rat, and, locally, the water rats. The local phrase had stuck and had long ago become a family name.

Just why Peter cultivated friendships with other species he couldn't say. His family deplored such contacts, so he tended to keep these visits to himself. His friend Tom knew of them and mildly disapproved, but shrugged his broad shoulders and didn't let it come between them.

Melvil rambled on awhile about his books. There wasn't much the old cat hadn't read. He was working his way through Trollope now, he said, the Barchester novels. He recommended them as soothing, and Peter thanked him, thinking to himself that tranquility was the last thing that he wanted at the moment.

"French's old hound had an accident, I heard?" It was clearly a request for information.

"I'm afraid so," Peter answered. "An assisted accident, I gather, though I know little of it. They say he'd become a menace." To put it mildly.

"Oh dear," was all that Melvil said.

"Good coffee."

"Yes, indeed. It was a birthday gift to Miss Lang from her niece in San Francisco. I've been quite appreciative, and very sparing in my use. She deserves her small pleasures."

"You like Miss Lang?"

"Oh yes, Peter. She's a fine person, though I say it who live by her generosity." He opened a cabinet door so that

Peter could see the wall of cans. "It's not so bad. I hold my nose and supplement it with table scraps when I may. I don't believe I could catch a mouse to save my life. No offense."

"None taken, Melvil. A field-mouse pie is fancied even by some rats. I've never tried it. I have more curiosity about mice than fellow feeling toward them, but I do sometimes question our callousness. Rats aren't bad creatures, but we're as species-centered as any other, I'm afraid."

"Inevitable, Peter, but your society produced *you*."

"An oddity." Peter shrugged and would have let the matter drop.

"I don't agree. If you don't mind my saying it, Peter, there is a grain of kindness in you that I believe runs through your race."

"It would be nice to think so," Peter said. "Rats have other faults."

"No doubt," the cat said dryly. "One marked quality of your own appears to be a restless curiosity. It's not the usual rodent failing, if it's a flaw at all."

Peter laughed. "My parents seem to think it is. Why shouldn't they?"

"Because, dear boy, though curiosity killed the careless cat, it generates momentum. I'm no sailor, but I understand there is such a thing as steerageway, the minimum of forward movement that is required to govern any ship. Few have it, Peter. Most of us are merely carried by the currents of our lives. On the other hand, of course, it requires you tend the tiller now and then. Where is it that you're bound?"

Peter shook his head. "I'm not sure, Melvil. I plan to

be a scientist like my father, and I enjoy my studies, but you're right. I'm restless these days. I want to do something, or go somewhere."

"And what stops you?"

"Everything, Melvil, you know that. Rats don't go off on pointless journeys, like lemmings rushing to the sea. I've even got my sister confused. Sara's very bright, and she doesn't know what to do with her life. I think she looks to me, Melvil, which isn't very helpful to her at the moment."

"I'm sure she looks up to you, Peter. You're a fine fellow. But you've said she writes stories?" Peter nodded. "Then she has a mind and an imagination of her own. Perhaps she'll be a writer, a grand calling"—Melvil beamed and looked toward the nearby bookshelves—"but with or without your help, she'll plot her life and live it. I wouldn't worry, Peter. You're young, and you're good-hearted. This is all simply the price of growing up to be someone. Just do your best, and you'll get through it. You'll go somewhere interesting as well, I'd wager. What was it, by the way, that you wanted to see me about?"

Peter smiled sheepishly. "What I've come about, Melvil, is radio."

"Indeed?" The cat smiled, too. "What aspect of the subject interests you?"

"Transmitting, receiving. Tom and I want to talk with my cousin Kendon at Cape End. I thought you might have something on it."

"Certainly," Melvil assured him, "something for every level of proficiency, I believe. I'm surprised that your father had nothing on his shelves."

"Not unless we were going to reinvent Marconi from

the point of view of contemporary electromagnetic theory. This seemed more efficient.''

"Yes, I suppose so. Stay here, Peter, and enjoy your coffee. I'll be back.''

Melvil returned in a few minutes, padding deftly on three legs, with several small volumes clutched in his other paw. "These should do. Try to get them back as soon as you can. You really must come and see us more often.''

"I will,'' said Peter, and he meant it. "Thank you for the books, and for the advice.''

"My pleasure, Peter.''

Peter tucked the books into his backpack and promised Melvil they'd have another chat when he returned them.

The old cat truly was a splendid creature. Peter wished he could ask Tom to come here with him. He'd like the cat. Tom was almost as much a reader as Melvil was. He should be a scholar, really. But Tom would come reluctantly, for he was too respectful of their old traditions. Lately even Tom had seemed uneasy, as if he were troubled by some worries of his own. Maybe discontent was catching, which was no joke, in fact. He'd have to talk with Tom about it.

Peter's friendship with Melvil had brought unexpected responsibilities. And benefits as well. Everything that Melvil said made sense, but what could a house cat really know of rats? Quite a lot, apparently. Peter mulled this over as he trotted home, and almost missed the musky scent of fox. He made a brief detour around the hunter.

·3·

Peter's calculus book lay unopened at his side. Calculus was interesting in itself, he felt. It was a satisfying exercise in logic, and he could see enough of his father's point about its usefulness in biological research to take the rest on trust. This was even his best time of day, the very crack of dawn, just light enough to read the words and symbols and see the elegant curves and functions. It was the time and place his mind was most awake, but it was also when the marsh around him came to life.

Peter stretched full-length along the cool, smooth stone that formed the porch before their den. The stone lay hidden in the weeds and wildflowers halfway up the little hill that rose some fifty feet from water's edge to wooded crown. The darkened entrance to the den was further sheltered by a jutting ledge of rock above. Peter felt it was the finest location on the Cape. The den itself began a dozen feet below. The narrow, winding entrance tunnel spilled into a paneled hall that always softly glowed with candle flames. Other dimly lighted corridors led on from there to many rooms and chambers, workshops, sculleries, and storage bins. A rat hole had a rhyme and reason of its own, to suit the interests of its inhabitants. Theirs was larger than they needed now, since Mother's brother Lucas left two years before, but they enjoyed the space and often filled it up with guests and friends. Rats were a sociable folk. Their successes as a race depended on both caution and collaboration. They worked together when they had to, without seeming to give up individualities. A peculiar species and a good one. Beyond the worth of having neighbors they could trust, they simply liked the company of other rats, to talk and eat and wander with and talk some more. All this drifted in and out of Peter's mind as the beauty of this summer dawn overwhelmed his good intentions.

The birds were up and out and rejoicing either at the day or at its good supply of gnats and flies. More power to them. A light sea breeze carried the rumpled sounds of surf across the marsh and brought the smells of salt and sand and seaweed to mingle with the lighter scents of wild roses and beach peas.

He'd do his reading later, when the sun had chased off more of the morning's cast of characters. He'd heard no one say so in as many words, but it seemed obvious to Peter that much of what they all did was aimed at making possible such times as this. If he never took a moment now and then to watch birds soaring in the morning breeze and sunlight touching silken grass tops, what was the point of all his industry?

Far off, no more than specks, a hawk plucked something living from the marsh. Peter lay and watched and let his mind run aimlessly among the little creeks and salt-grass islands of the marsh and beyond the dawn-lit clouds. Gradually his thoughts dissolved until his senses briefly merged with sounds and colors, smells, and touch of wind on fur.

What was that? What had brought him back to the porch and stone? There was no one here except himself. Suddenly he'd had enough of nature. He was nature, *Rattus norvegicus*, rodent and social animal par excellence, and at the moment a student of calculus. He picked up his book and opened it to chapter 3.

He was deeply tangled in infinity an hour later when his father appeared with a steaming mug of coffee.

"Hard at work, I see. That's good. The coffee's done."

"Morning, Father." Peter put down his book and disappeared into the tunnel, to reemerge in half a minute with his cup.

"Nice day," his father observed.

"Wonderful day," Peter agreed. "I wish I could go for a ramble."

"Hmm, a little risky. A day like this one brings out hikers and sends bird-watchers with binoculars to the overlook. They won't want to see you, Peter, handsome fellow that you are."

Peter laughed. "No, and they'd just stink up the field again with poisoned bait. It's so lovely in the light, though." He looked up at a large white cloud, its bottom tinted artistically with umber, solid-seeming and keeping its curious if senseless shape as it moved with solemn speed across the sky.

"It is that," his father agreed. He was a scientist and physician and spent long hours in his laboratory, working as he had for years on a study of the immune system. "More benefit to the next generation than this one, Son," Grandfather had observed. "Most likely," Father had said. Morning coffee on the porch was a never-failing ritual, however, and office hours of a sort for his own family. He could sit happily in silence, drink his coffee and watch the marsh, or he could talk.

"If you have any problems with that exercise, come and see me in the lab. I'm just writing up some notes this morning."

"Okay, thanks," Peter said. "I may not have to. It's pretty interesting stuff."

"Mmm, yes. It may all be random in the end, of course, but on the way it makes a pretty pattern. Whether you see it in the wind waves through the grass or in your book," he added. He looked at his son a moment and smiled with a warmth he rarely showed, as if they had just shared an important secret. One of the sweet mysteries of life, perhaps, as Peter's little sister had once observed excitedly of some small wonder.

After more coffee and a roll with cherry jam, alone in the kitchen before the household was awake, Peter went to his room to work. He liked a big breakfast, too, but it could take half the morning, and he didn't have the time today. Unlike the field and marsh, he barely saw his room, though he had spent much of his life within its walls and had made it his with paint and pictures. It was a large room, and why not, when size was only a matter of a little extra tunneling. The rats had mastered the engineering of cave structures some millennia before, the science of supports and stresses, rock mechanics, soils, and vents and drains. They did this on their own and based on independent investigations of chemistry and physics. The borrowings from humans came later.

The rough plaster walls of Peter's room were painted white and hung with drawings, bits of driftwood, and other objects that once had caught his fancy: a barrel stave, a piece of fishing net with colored floats, and Appleton the rattlesnake, the grisly gift of a playmate who'd been ordered to dispose of it. In a place of honor, where he could see it from his bed, was a watercolor of the marsh and dunes and sea and sky as seen from their own porch. His mother had painted it at his innocent request when he was young, and it served him better than a window on the world above.

He worked in silence except for the scratching of his pencil and an internal colloquy with ghosts named Archimedes, Newton, and Laplace. Only the faint aroma of fish chowder drifting down many feet of corridor finally broke his concentration.

"Lunch!" His brother John's small voice came through the partly open door. Meals were taken seriously among the water rats, too seriously Peter sometimes thought, but he enjoyed his food as much as anyone.

When he appeared in the kitchen no more than five minutes later, it was empty, except for a large pot of chowder simmering on the stove. A note propped up at his place read, "Peter, join us for a picnic on the ledge. Rolls in the oven and chowder in the pot. Love, Mother." Peter smiled. After his father's warnings against going out in daylight, they were having a family picnic at high noon. He ladled chowder into a mug, retrieved two whole-wheat rolls, and headed for the lower tunnel. This was an escape route really, in the unlikely event of an invasion of wolverines presumably, but it was customary among rats. It was rarely used, as little of interest to them lay directly south, but it was a convenient route to their favorite picnic rock. That was a hefty boulder, guarded from the footpath above and the sand below by brambles and a thick growth of poison ivy.

"Here's the scholar," said his grandfather. "Could use a bit of brain food by now, I'd think?"

"Yes, sir. That's a good book, though. It's hard going, but it's all there. He hasn't left out the crucial point the way they often do."

"Um-hmm," Grandfather nodded approvingly from behind his mug. Unless there was a more obvious reference, there was rarely any doubt who *they* might be—their dominant and domineering senior partners on the planet. They were the cornucopia of technology and theory, art and music, that had long enriched the life of every rat, and they were equally the source of nearly all the rats' fears for the present and the future. They were the authors of countless works of speculation that ran on faulty logic and brilliant bounds of faith, like recipes for chowder that left out the fish. There had always been some tension between those rats who made full use of human knowledge and those who still resisted its temptations, but all the old traditions counseled caution, and the boldest rat could see the sense in looking twice before leaping.

"Sailboat," said his sister, Sara, pointing out beyond the line of surf.

"A beauty," agreed her little brother, John. "I wish we had one."

19

No one answered this wistful comment, so Sara said, "Me, too," and John looked at her with fond appreciation. Peter knew enough to change the subject.

"Burry says there's fewer boats running out of Stone Harbor this year."

"Running out of fish, most likely," Father said. He shook his head, but left it at that.

Peter let it go as well. This whole business of the world's resources was a new concern for rats, one that had gradually surfaced in his own short lifetime, and they didn't know yet what to make of it. It would take many late-night conversations before they had a glimmer, probably. He could see it looming. Not to face at lunch, however.

"Do you want to use the lab this afternoon, Peter?" One of his father's firm beliefs was that for safety and precision, lab work should be mostly solitary.

"No, sir. I promised Tom I'd help him finish the new tunnel. He's almost through." He also wanted to take Tom the books on radio.

"That's nice of you, Peter," his mother said. "I've worried about Mason crossing the road with his rheumatism. I'm sure the new tunnel will be a help to them." Worrying about her neighbors was one of Mother's principal concerns, and it was often just enough to set the needed help in motion. Did rats find their niche, already made, or did they draw their lives around them to fashion one that fit? He'd done neither yet, for all his studying.

"Healthy work," Grandfather mused. "Does no harm to get up a muck sweat now and then. Smile, if you will, my boy. I've dug my share of tunnels."

"Yes, sir, I know." More than his share, probably, but still it was amusing and ironic coming from the fastidious old rat, always groomed and polished and generally sunk back in his easy chair, from where he issued kind but firm instructions to his patient family.

Sara had said nothing since her observation on the boat, but she listened carefully, Peter knew. It was odd that he didn't worry much about upsetting his elders with his often-challenging remarks but cared far more what Sara thought. He knew she looked up to him, and he felt the weight of that responsibility. There was a line, he'd begun to realize, between his parents and himself that was something more than simply membership in different generations. Young rats and old should merge almost imperceptibly, and he should be already nearly one with them in dealing with the world. But he saw changes in the land about them that they often didn't seem to see, hairline fractures in the web of time that threatened to grow larger. He'd spoken little of this yet to anyone, not even Tom.

They talked on of tunnels, highways, gardens, and a whole catalog of physical infirmities, while Peter listened and enjoyed the pleasant combination of cool breezes and warm sun on an exquisite summer day. The flitting, in the grass below, of bright-green dragonflies had filled his vision, and his thoughts soared far beyond the marsh in calculated curves.

"Tunneler?" His mother touched him gently on the arm.

"Oh . . . ? Yes," he answered sheepishly. He saw his sister grinning.

·4·

Peter set off for Tom's by a route that threaded the old
hardwood forest on the hill above and skirted Maple
Swamp amid the briars and bracken at its borders. There
were walkers on the trail this afternoon. He could see the
patches of bright color through the trees and hear the cries
of children, the most charming and dangerous of creatures.
They had eyes that looked in all the shadows.

Tom's father greeted Peter at the entrance to the den.
He was enjoying an after-lunch cigar and counting swallows, he said. There were plenty still, he added with a
laugh. Mason was pretty-well retired now from his work
as a cabinetmaker, more because of crippled paws than
simply age. The Waterrats' handsome dining table and
long sideboard were from his workshop years ago, and
some of Father's laboratory cabinets as well.

Tom did nearly all the work these days, with admirable
care and skill. "To each according to his need and from
each according to his abilities," an old rats' rule that was

sometimes aped by men. Perhaps it simply wasn't possible for them.

"You'll find Tom down in the hole. It's good of you to help us, Peter."

"It's a pleasure, Mason," Peter assured him, and it was. Aside from the good feeling of being useful, he liked to dig. He liked getting hot and dirty and stretching his muscles and then getting clean again and resting from some job well done.

"Tom?"

"Who else?" Tom had had his fill of digging and was glad the project was nearly finished.

"You can't tell it just by looking at you," Peter answered cheerfully. "Some sort of inept groundhog, maybe."

"Be my guest." Tom brushed dirt off his nose and handed Peter a shiny spade. "I'll haul a bit."

"Righto," Peter said, and went to work. Tom moved dirt and rocks in a barrower, a four-wheeled cart that had been designed eons in the past for just this purpose by some rodent genius whose name had characteristically been lost.

The ground was good beneath the field—no need for supports, except the usual safety chambers at five-foot intervals. The tunnel advanced two feet, then five, until Tom called a halt.

"Let's run the line again." Tom sighted through a transit from the last marker and called off directions to Peter for driving in the stake. They unrolled a measuring tape. "That's done it," Tom concluded with satisfaction. "We'll take it up from here in a right-hand spiral."

It was another half hour before Peter's shovel struck

23

stone, and it took ten minutes more to break through to the surface at the bushy backside of a boulder. A little paring and cleaning, and they were done. Tunnels were designed for strength, not beauty. "A rustic decor" was the usual ironic designation of their necessarily low profile. But in fact, a well-crafted tunnel had a beauty of its own, Peter decided. As they loaded the picks and shovels in the barrower and made their way back to the den, he considered how very little meddling with the planet was needed to produce utility and even beauty. Their civilization was sophisticated and complex, and yet it sat lightly on the land. The bucket of a power shovel could sweep away a den, but it would grow again within a week, like some bedouin encampment.

They showered mud and sand from their coats and then plunged into the bathing pool. The clear water, a constant seventy degrees year round, felt cool and refreshing after their hot work. In winter it provided steamy comfort for freezing limbs and paws.

"Thanks again, Peter."

"My pleasure, Tom, really. Any time," he added, laughing.

"A pretty safe offer," Tom agreed, with a smile. "We now have at least two more entrances than any other hole on the Cape. Still, it will be handy for Dad. He stiffened up once last winter smack in the middle of the road. Nothing coming, luckily."

"I got the books, Tom. I haven't had a chance to look at them, but I brought them in my pack."

"Great," Tom said. "You're not going to tempt me into becoming a scientist," he added.

"Hardly—just a little better informed. You humanists live on the same planet and by the same physical laws as we ordinary citizens. You'd find it handy to know about these things."

"Then it's good I have a friend who'll tell me what I need to know. I'll read the books. I find science entertaining, Peter, honestly. I enjoy the nonsense of an intricate machine without a purpose or a switch to turn it on or off."

"And no suspicion there might be an artist behind so much artistry?"

"Merely a suspicion." Tom floated peacefully on his back, dead-rat fashion, his eyes closed and his whiskers twitching.

"I smell mushrooms," Peter said.

"Stuffed mushrooms," Tom agreed with pleasure. "With fresh crab, garlic, bread crumbs, and olive oil. If you'd care to stay for supper . . ." It wasn't even a rhetorical question. No rat could pass up a dish like that, even without an afternoon of gritty labor.

Peter swam a dozen pool lengths at top speed and then dried and fluffed his fur and hung his big towel on a wooden peg.

"Are you still that full of energy?" Tom asked. "Sorry we're out of projects for the moment."

"I just feel good," Peter said. He did, and for once he didn't care to analyze his thoughts. Whatever else life brought, there were these strange good moments now and then.

"Your mom's the best cook around."

"You're telling me. Just look at us." It was true that

Tom's family were all big rats, but they weren't fat, really, not even his father, who had sensibly cut back his eating as he worked less.

They sat on the stoop outside the entrance to the den and looked through Peter's books in the still-strong evening light. Tom's father had supplied two slim cigars from his valued stock, and both friends puffed contentedly as they absorbed the basic concepts of electronics and confirmed their understanding by comparing books and talking through ideas. A lot of learning could be solitary, but you only knew you knew something when you could speak about it sensibly. *Transistor* and *capacitor* and *diode*, fair Diode, goddess of the gateway; they were all words with good Greek and Latin roots and bore the sort of solid facts that appealed to rodent minds.

"We'll have to make a supply run to the dump," Tom said.

"Um, guess so." Peter had mixed feelings about the dump, and mixed memories. It was a place of fascination, a window on the best and worst of human machinations. It was also a gathering place for predators and vermin. Crazy Duane lived there in an abandoned ice-cream truck. He'd once frightened Peter half to death. Rats went mad like other creatures, and these poor fellows were often the ones seen and killed by humans. Not so many, though, for all but the worst could be helped or cured with drugs. Churlish sea gulls always stood about in gangs at any dump and mocked any other creatures that appeared. They were sane enough, but thoroughly nasty birds. If the summer renters could hear them talk, they'd not find them so attractive, Peter reckoned. Fortunately, at night they went to sea.

At the dump, however, he and Tom would find everything they needed. Piles of radios and sound equipment, computers even, wire and metal, all discarded because of some small failure that the owner couldn't fix or trust a shop to mend for less than the cost of something new. Dumps had been the beginning of it all, of course, of the rats' peculiar intellectual parasitism on the human race. Rats had salvaged their first potsherds from the kitchen middens at Ur of the Chaldeans, and it had gone on from there. Well, nothing ventured, nothing gained, thought Peter, which was not a Rattish maxim in the least.

·5·

Tom curled up later that evening with *More Radio Made Easy*. It wouldn't have been his first choice of bedtime reading. He had a stack of history books on his table, some Rattish and some human. There was a small pile of mysteries as well, all human of course, for the whole idea of mystery appeared a bit perverse to the average rat. Life was mysterious enough, most rats seemed to feel, without setting out to make it more so. Or so they said. Tom wasn't the only rat who liked these stories. It was Peter's mother who'd loaned him his first thriller.

More Radio Made Easy wouldn't have been his choice at any time, but he'd promised Peter. It was interesting enough, just ingredients and processes really, like cabinet-making or a recipe for carrot cake. And Peter was right that he should know a little about such things, simply to have a well-rounded mind. He read some more.

Peter could be very persuasive. Tom knew he could hold

out against his arguments if he had to, but usually it just wasn't worth the effort. They would build the radio and put up the antenna, a risky task he wasn't looking forward to, and they'd talk to Kendon. Kendon outdid even Peter in some ways. The one time the family had come down from North Cape for a visit, Kendon had just about swept them all away with talk of electrons and atomic nuclei. Peter had been fascinated by Kendon's energy and by how much he seemed to know. Kendon had talked with Peter's father, too, almost as an equal, and Tom had just hung around in the background and finally excused himself and gone home. But that was over a year ago. They'd grown up a little in between. Kendon might be all right by now.

Enough of radio. He had too many unanswered questions finally, and it had all begun to blur. He eyed his pile of books with satisfaction. It wasn't late. He still had time to read a couple of chapters on the British Empire. That was the sort of thing he really liked, events with plot and motivation, of long-enough ago to be well documented but not so ancient that the records had been lost or fuddled. History was another of his more peculiar interests, a kind of mystery on a larger scale. Rats valued humans chiefly for their science, and to a lesser degree their music and their art. Even human lives and literatures were interesting to some, for human minds were molded by the same forces that nurtured theirs. The broad sweep of human history, however, seemed almost ludicrous to many rats, a rowdy burlesque of civilized existence. It appeared to Tom that it was more. There was massive stupidity, of course, but also a great deal of struggling with complex realities. Rats prided themselves on a long tradition of simple living and good sense, but the more Tom learned of humans, the more he saw the depth of the rats' dependence on them. He wished he had the time to read, to understand.

He did like working in his father's shop. He'd learned the crafts of carpentry and cabinetmaking well. He hadn't had to choose the family trade, but he was an only child, and it had so clearly pleased his parents. His work was good; his father said so. There was satisfaction in finding the right piece of wood, matching grains, and making a perfect cut or joint. There was a lot of satisfaction, but not fulfillment. His heart just wasn't in it. His father knew that, and it saddened him. Someone had to do the work, of course, and he had the knowledge and the skills. He had the size and strength, as well, to do things easily that his father had struggled with. So long as he could read, his life was good.

He fell asleep with the lamp still bright and his book slipping from his paws. His mother saw him as she passed. She smiled and shook her head. She turned down his light and closed the book and put it on the table. *British India?* Gracious, and such a tome. It would have waked them all if it had fallen in the night.

Tom didn't wake, but he slept uneasily, and shortly before dawn he had a dream. He knew it was a dream because he'd had it several times before, and it was as much a memory. He and Peter were small again and had found their way into a darkened supermarket. At first they roamed the aisles in amazement and delight, but as each enticing smell was overlaid by still another, Tom's poor stomach began to rumble like a dragon's, and Peter heard and shushed him with a grin. Worse, Tom started drooling. They couldn't touch a thing, of course. It was the trial of Tantalus in an A&P. For it was bad enough they'd taken risks to little purpose; the prohibitions against troubling the humans were as old, he guessed, as the flints and bones at Olduvai. Tom's agony was ended by a cat, the size of a refrigerator as he remembered it. They froze, quite literally, behind the milk and butter until the creature went the other way and they could reach the window in the store- room. Tom woke at dawn in a clammy sweat and wondered why just now he'd had this dream of fruitless longing when his life was pleasant and his spirit usually at peace.

·6·

Sara was surprised when she saw Peter leave the den and start across the field. She hadn't wanted to startle her brother in the dark, and then the moment passed and he was out of sight. Or was there something slightly furtive in his leaving that had stopped her? Caution was second nature for any rat, but there was a subtle difference between care and stealth. Tom and Peter had been up to something with wires and solder all that week, and Sara had grown curious, but had been too proud to ask.

She leaped down from her favorite evening refuge on the still-warm rock and followed her brother into the grassy tunnels that led toward Maple Swamp and the pine woods beyond. He was probably going to see Tom. Just for fun, and because she wasn't ready to go inside and start her reading, she'd see if she could track him there. It wouldn't be that easy, for Peter had eyes and ears as good as any fox. She moved fast and silently along the path, hoping to catch a glimpse of his long shadow or hear a rustle in the grass ahead. His scent hung faintly in the breeze, but a scent trail wasn't reliable in the damp night air.

Peter would think it foolish, but he'd never know. He'd better not. It was hard enough to be two years younger. To be caught at some childish trick like this would be far worse. She wasn't even sure why she was doing it.

The night held no special fears for her, fewer than the daylight for a water rat. There were owls, of course, but the greatest danger was from dogs and humans, and these were safely settled by their own hearths now. Night was Sara's time, night and the lovely hours of dusk and dawn when rats could see the world but stay masked in shadows.

Peter's scent was faint but present, and then she saw a darker blackness cross a patch of starlight just before the path plunged down through pungent cedars and onto the rangers' tanbark trail. The cedars ended abruptly at the edge of the swamp where the larger and much older maples spread their gnarled branches wide over the dark pools and waterways.

Sara stepped onto the boardwalk with the same feeling of boldness that always accompanied any invasion of human territory. She could hear the faint thrum of Peter's paws on the planks not far ahead. She padded almost silently herself, catching the rhythm of the cool smooth boards and moving fast again. The swamp was best at night. By day it slept, and the strollers looked in vain for its inhabitants, finding no more than a token turtle or the odd foolhardy frog. Another time she would have stopped and stretched out on one of the log benches and waited, barely breathing, until the swamp creatures forgot her and continued with their businesses.

Peter trotted on, unhurried now, but wasting no time on the pleasures of the swamp. He had something else in mind apparently, and she wasn't entirely surprised that he passed the turn to Tom's and headed west toward the road. She had to wait until he had cleared the long culvert that led beneath the highway, for he could have heard her within its echoing walls as well as she heard him. There was a moment of panic at the other end. She'd torn breakneck through the pipe, but there was no sign of Peter. Stone Harbor was his most likely destination. A few yards down that path, however, and all trace of Peter's scent had gone. Turning back, she made a wide half circle through the weeds and found the trail again, going south now toward Great Pond. Why there? Really she should give it up, a silly business anyway, hardly ratlike to follow someone for no good reason other than on a kind of private dare. But now she was too curious to quit. *Moby Dick* could wait until another night.

Whoa! She'd almost blown it then. He was just ahead on the narrow path, moving cautiously and stopping every few feet to listen. He stopped again just before the trees came to an end at the large freshwater kettle pond. The tall grass creaked momentarily, and two large forms joined Peter on the path. Raccoons!

Sara felt the hair on her neck rise, and her heart beat faster. Not that raccoons were to be feared. They went their way, and the rats went another. There were many similarities in their tastes and habits, so it was hardly an accident if their paths rarely crossed. What was Peter up to? No wonder he'd seemed stealthy. Now more than ever she ought to go back, and more than ever she was drawn by curiosity to stay.

Peter and the two raccoons talked a moment in low voices and then went forward to the pond. At its edge a small boat had been pulled up on the sandy beach by its human owners, a child's boat almost. The raccoons began to push it toward the water. Worse and worse. If any of the unwritten prohibitions that guided their lives loomed largest, it was the one against unnecessary interference with the humans. The humans knew the rats were there, but they knew almost nothing about their lives, and they were usually content to let them be, so long as they weren't forced to confront the evidence. "What they don't want to see can't hurt us," as the graybeards put it.

What was Peter doing? He was a good and cooperative son and a kind and thoughtful older brother, but in his quiet way, he was a rebel. He had challenged Grandfather's wisdom more than once, respectfully, of course, and to the old rat's satisfaction usually. "Why?" "Because it was always so." "But why so, Grandfather?" And on it went. But this was different.

"What have we here?" She almost leaped from her skin at the sound of the low, rough voice behind her and whirled like lightning with her small fangs bared. A third raccoon stood in the path, looking amused, she thought, unless his faint smirk was the usual expression on the faces of these supercilious-appearing beasts.

"You're late, miss. Peter, do you perhaps know who this is?"

"This is my sister, Sara," Peter said, as if he were introducing them at a garden party. He really was a prince sometimes.

"Pleased to meet you," the raccoon rumbled in a not-unfriendly way. Peter, too, seemed more amused than angry, but that almost made it worse. Utter honesty was called for.

"Sorry, Peter, I don't know why I followed you. Just to see if I could, I think, and then I got curious."

"It's all right," Peter said. He looked quizzically at the raccoons, who made vague gestures that seemed to indicate indifference at least. "Come with us if you like. We'll just do some fishing. We won't be late." He really seemed to mean it.

"Okay," she said. "I'd like to." She leaped onto the stern seat of the little dinghy while two of the raccoons pushed them off into the quiet pond. A faint breeze barely ruffled the surface of the water, leaden in the light of a rising moon, but it was enough to dilute and dissipate the sound of their oars and the soft, deep voices of the fishermen.

"Pole, um."

"Bait, um."

"Yar."

Peter and the younger raccoons fished. The larger animal who had surprised her on the trail did all the rowing. They were a father and his sons, she learned, and obviously experienced fishermen. Peter had been with them before, it seemed.

"Got 'im." The raccoon beside her began to reel in a good-sized fish that plunged and pulled and zigzagged wildly as it neared the surface. It landed in the boat below her and began to thrash. Without thinking, she bit it hard at the back of the head, and it lay quiet on the planking.

The old one smiled at her and grunted approvingly, and Sara felt foolishly proud.

When a dozen big white perch lay in the bottom of the boat, the oarsman pulled for shore.

"Your first time fishing from a boat?" he asked. Now that the serious business was attended to, they could talk more freely, she supposed.

"Yes, sir," Sara replied, and there were quiet guffaws from the other raccoons.

"Never mind them, miss. They've no respect for age nor wisdom. You can call me Murray."

"Thank you, Murray. It was fun."

"Nice way to spend an evening, that's sure. You'll find those fish fine eating, too. Nothing sweeter than white perch with mushrooms and wild onions. Yum."

"Stop it, Dad," one of the fishermen laughed. "I'm ready to eat them raw right now."

Peter and Sara thanked the raccoons and said good night. They each carried two big perch, cleaned and scaled, but still a fair weight of fish across their backs.

"They're good-hearted fellows." Peter seemed to feel a need to explain himself. "I've fished with them a few times before, and Murray and I have talked a little. They don't have much in the way of culture, but they're no fools."

"I liked them, Peter. They were so calm and kind, and the older one was sweet. They're not so different from rats, are they?"

"Not so, not in the important things. I know it's against our customs."

"I wouldn't say anything, Peter."

"I know you won't. It isn't that. I don't . . . I wouldn't want you to think I don't respect the traditions. But nothing stays entirely the same, not even rats."

"I guess," said Sara.

"Or that I'd encourage you to break the rules."

"No, Peter."

"I'm glad you liked them. They liked you. They seem rough, but they like quiet, thoughtful souls. Old Murray tells stories, wonderful long tales about their ancestors and their past. What you'd expect really, about dogs and fish and all, but with a lot more perception than you might think, and more poetry. They know that pond down to its toenails. He'd probably tell you a story."

"I'd like that. I could write it down."

"Um-hmm."

And then, of course I'd have to explain where I heard it, like where we got the perch, she thought. They finished the journey in silence. She said good night to her brother in the entrance hall and went to take a quick dip in the bathing pool while Peter stowed the fish. They would make a good breakfast for them all in the morning.

She read a little, but her mind was too full of her strange evening to take in the complexity of Melville's characters. In the morning, maybe. She closed the book and speculated on the probable contents of raccoon epics: narrow escapes, maybe; famous raids on garbage dumps; the Great White Perch. Did it matter, so long as it meant something to them? She'd like to hear one. Oh dear, she'd done something against the rules and, worse, against common sense that said keep to your own kind and never blunder around the countryside unnecessarily, and worse still, she couldn't quite feel guilty. Peter might not ask her to go with him again, not for a while, but she'd been this time, and it would be a little different between them now. And some-day she would have a real adventure. She slept and dreamed of boats and giant fish.

·7·

Sara carried a brimming cup of hot coffee up the dark
sandy tunnel to the entrance of the den. Her younger
brother, John, was there already, stretched out on the sun-
warmed stone and gazing across the salt marsh toward the
dunes of the outer beach and the ocean beyond. The sea
was choppy and deep blue in the morning light.

"Hi."

"Hello."

She settled herself just inside the protection of the overhanging grass. There were few hawks aloft at this time of
day, but a rat's first thought was generally of cover.

"What's up?"

"Birds and bugs mostly. The blackbirds are chasing a
snake across the field." He pointed to a flurry of the dark
birds, hovering and diving repeatedly at their unseen target.

"Good for them."

"It's just a little snake."

40

"If it eats enough blackbird eggs, it could get to be a big one, though."

"Um."

Um indeed. Leave it to John to be on the side of the snake. Rats were all naturalists of necessity. The more you knew about the habits of your neighbors, the better off you were. But John's interest went deeper and had since the days she'd held him on her lap and pointed out the swallows making high-speed attacks on flies and mosquitoes. Once he had followed an ant across the field in daylight and been saved from a hawk only by Peter's speed and daring. He had long ago exhausted Sara's knowledge of the natural world, and it was he and Peter who now made occasional forays into the swamp to observe old friends and add to the list of species they had identified. It was an important interest, of course, and if John already knew what he was doing with his life . . . well, good for him.

She wasn't sure what she was doing. Doing her schoolwork as well as she could, reading a lot of books, and visiting her friends. It was all right—fine, really. She liked her family and her life, but she'd begun seriously to wonder what was next.

"What are you reading?"

"A novel about a whale. You'd like it someday, but not yet."

"Oh. But you like it?"

"Uh-huh. It's strange. The characters aren't like the people we've listened to from under the boardwalk. They think. They feel things. They're a lot like rats in many ways, except that they seem quite mad much of the time."

"Oh." John's attention had returned to the blackbirds,

who had managed to divert the snake from the thicket where their nests were hidden. Hidden in theory, anyway; the snake knew they were there.

There was a faint rustle beyond the large gray stone that lay a little down the slope from them and which at times held gulls and terns and occasionally a confused chipmunk risking death to sight a familiar tree. Her father appeared on its still-shadowed side and with a quick look skyward joined them on the porch.

"Up early, youngsters."

"Not as early as you, Father," Sara said.

"Malinda's boy had a fall. Bruised some ribs. They thought he might have broken them. The little idiot was playing tag or something at the top of a full-grown elm. I sometimes think this generation has lost its senses." But he was smiling as he said it. "Do I smell fish?"

"Yes, Peter got some." With a little help, she thought. This may be difficult. "Mom's cooking them."

The snake by now had reached the safety of the blackberry thicket, and the birds had returned to their gossiping above the nest bush.

A dozen feet below the entrance, in the big kitchen of the Waterrats' rambling den, the smell of frying perch was mouth-watering. Sara's mother and grandmother were cooking potatoes and onions to go with the fish. Grandfather was already at the table.

"Ah, Sara. How's the whale hunt?" For an awful moment she thought he meant her expedition of the night before.

"Good. I like it. I even like the parts about cetology. Ahab's mad, isn't he?"

"Maybe. Maybe they're all mad, but they can write.

That was my favorite book when I was a boy. I wanted to go to sea for quite a while.''

"You, Grandfather?'' Her grandfather was a physician like her father, and like Peter, too, in a few years, and maybe even like her someday. And usually he was the spokesman for tradition, for "a hundred million years of watching your tail,'' as Peter put it.

"But I came to my senses, as you see. A grand book, though. I'm glad you like it. Peter, my lad, where'd you find these plump fish? Not under a bush, I'd imagine.''

"No, sir. Some friends caught more than they could use.''

"And were poaching on Great Pond, eh? Say no more.''

Nicely done, thought Sara, and a lucky break at that, but it still bothered her. She liked being straight with everyone, and she was just beginning to understand that even with the best of will it wasn't always possible. A disconcerting thought. Father, at least, wasn't fooled. She'd seen him smile when Grandfather asked about the perch. Probably her mother wondered, too, but she wouldn't ask.

"Some of the Fort Hill families have seafaring blood,'' Grandfather went on, "rats right off old Putterman's whalers when he left the sea and built his house a hundred years ago. They're still a restless crew.'' He shook his head, in disapproval, presumably, but Sara couldn't be entirely sure. She loved her grandfather and knew that she was a special favorite of his, but she was in awe of him as well. He was the patriarch of their small family. Small by water rat standards, at least. Grandfather had upped burrow and moved when he and Grandmother were still young, to fill the need for a physician at mid-Cape. Besides their immediate family, only Uncle Lucas lived nearby.

Grandfather was no autocrat. Rats made their important decisions by consensus—and after careful thought and much polite discussion. But aged rats were respected, and particularly when they were filled with wisdom and learning, as Grandfather was.

"Must have been a hard life for them. The heat, the cold; they'd eat no better than the crew sometimes, but they survived."

"I didn't know you had such fondness for the old sea dogs, Dad." Father sounded amused. Grandfather was hardly a romantic.

"Hey? No shame in strength and courage, Son. They were immigrants, escaping from conditions even humans wouldn't bear. Only a fool goes out in boats when he doesn't have to."

"You'll eat lobster quick enough when Alfred brings us some."

"If Alfred wants to risk his tail, the least we can do is show appreciation. More coffee in that pot, Nan?"

Mother refilled his cup. You just never knew with Grandfather. Sara had been afraid to look up after that remark about boats. Now she glanced at Peter, who appeared as cool and cheerful as ever. She looked at the three of them, her grandfather, her father, and her brother: big, sleek water rats, Grandfather heavier and grayer but still hale and strong. They were all three smart and a little arrogant and kind. All individuals as well: Grandfather the genial family doctor, as near retirement as a rat ever gets; Father more a scientist when he had the chance; and Peter just partway through his studies, though she already thought of him as bearing the torch, or whatever that odd thing was—the staff of Aesculapius. The humans had such peculiar minds. She was smart, too, and she could be a doctor if she chose to be, and if she worked at it hard enough, but was that what she wanted? She had time, but it had begun to weigh on her.

"Sara, I'd like you to take these books over to Lucas's this afternoon and invite them to supper. We're getting steamers from old Henry. And Peter, I'll want you to help your father get them after sundown."

"Glad to, Mother. Will there be enough for me to invite Tom? He loves clams."

"Enough even for Tom, I'd think. In fact, he might help fetch them. That way we'll be sure to have plenty."

Neat, Sara thought. What a good day this was turning out to be. A visit to Luc and clams and Tom coming. Tom was big and always used the longest words he could, but he was fun and really rather nice.

She helped her grandmother with the breakfast dishes, a particularly spectacular pile of greasy plates and fish bones. Just her luck, but Grandmother so clearly enjoyed the task of turning dirty pots and plates into clean ones that Sara soon forgot to fuss. Her grown-ups seemed to look on any work as such a privilege that it was hard not to want to join in. She knew how to scrub a pot at least. She must have passed some test a while ago, for no one checked her work. She dried the plates while Grandmother washed and rinsed them, and she piled them carefully in the cupboard.

"Such nice old dishes. I never really noticed them before, Grandmother."

Grandmother smiled. "No reason you should, dear. They've been here for you always, like the den and the sun and the sea. They're just old capeware from the works at Towset, long gone now. I hate to see one break, and they don't last forever if you use them, but why have them otherwise?''

How did Grandmother make her feel so good by saying such simple things? Sara always felt her worth and her belonging when she was with her. She and Grandmother had picked raspberries the week before, and it had seemed a timeless and reaffirming ritual. The pies they'd made from the berries helped, too, with crusts that crumbled into luscious flakes almost as they touched your tongue. Grandmother knew the family recipes and the family tree by heart, the spiderweb of relationships between third cousins twice removed. She looked surprised but pleased when Sara kissed her on the cheek before she hung up her towel and went to start her morning studies.

The sun and the sea. Sara had so much. It seemed terribly greedy of her to want more. She did, though.

·8·

Uncle Lucas lived a ways across the field, in a pleasant hole beneath an errant boulder. This rock sat very near the edge of the small bluff that directly overlooked the salt marsh itself. It had sat there for some time, as Lucas pointed out, long enough to collect furrows where the Nausets had shaped their bows and arrows centuries before. It was nearer now to plunging into the marsh, "but not so near as some of us," Luc said.

He had recently married and was the most relaxed and least eccentric he had been in Sara's memory of him and was still one of her favorite relatives. Luc was a publisher and a printer and was known beyond the Cape for the beauty and high quality of his work. He preferred to publish Rattish writings, but these were few, so most of his productions were of human origin in a variety of tongues. There were almost no translations, as rats learned languages quite easily and saw little point in diluting precisely the experience they sought in books. He was a musician, too, a violinist of local fame, who played with small ensembles up and down the Middle Cape. In fact, the more musically inclined knew Lucas as a fiddler who made books. It hardly mattered. Neither role defined his character, or earned him a penny, any more than Father's or Grandfather's doctoring did for them. There were no fees or obligations among the rats and no professions, really, but simply dedication to a calling and to the knowledge it required. It made things both simpler and more difficult, Sara decided, than for the humans who were so concerned with labels and credentials. It was all on *you* with rats, at times a heavy burden.

The field at midday was calm and lovely, seen through a golden haze of summer grasses. The fragrance of the wildflowers was overpowering. Sara knew it hid her own faint scent. Only the bees were about and busy, and they paid her no attention. The sky was empty, but she kept watch on it. A speck could become a deadly missile in a few seconds, hard to escape once it held you in its eye, unless there was a handy hole. She smelled Luc's pipe some yards from the rock. Few rats smoked, though it apparently did them little harm, one of the many small biological advantages they held over their human neighbors. Grandfather loved his calabash, and Peter and Tom puffed cigars when they could get them, and looked properly foolish, she felt. Luc's pipe was as constant a companion as his violin.

"Luc," she called softly from a dozen feet away.

"Sara? Come along. I was thinking about you."

"You were?" she asked. It still surprised and pleased her when Luc took an interest in her life and doings.

"I made you something." He handed her a small leather-bound volume with a strap and fastener. She opened it and saw it was a journal, a blank one with soft, faintly lined pages and a place in the spine to hold a pen.

"Oh, Luc, it's lovely. I'm to write in it?"

"Well, that's not for me to decide," he said with a smile, "but I thought you might like to, that you might have the inclination and want to take the time."

"Thank you, Luc." She held the volume for a moment and then put it carefully in her bag. She hardly knew what to say. From Luc it was more than a gift, it was an invitation and an expression of confidence as well. She liked to write, of course. She enjoyed composing letters to her cousins and even essays for school, anything really. A note for the kitchen table was a chance to play with words. She'd always written stories, for herself and just for fun, and she told wild tales to John, silly fantasies about talking clams and mice. Luc apparently had something more in mind. But a writer was someone who. . . .

"How's Melville?"

"Fine. Why does everyone want to know, Luc? Grandfather asked, too, and then he went on about the Putterman rats and the sea and all."

"Good question, and I don't know really. *Moby Dick* is the great American novel, along with *Huckleberry Finn.* The wildness of nature and the nobility of the common man. Why do rats care, though? We're common enough, of course, no dukes and duchesses, and lord knows we float on the untamed sea of the natural world, if we're not submerged entirely in it. What do Huck and Ishmael have in common, do you think?"

Sara thought a minute. Luc's questions always challenged her, without ever seeming to threaten her self-confidence.

"They're just . . . It's common sense. They see things clearly and react with sense, the way you and I would."

"The way we hope we would, anyway. As any sane rat would want to. Yes, I think so. Good sense and generosity and humor, maybe, and an understanding of their own place in things, as neither king nor pawn. It isn't Melville they're interested in, Sara. It's you."

"Ah," said Sara, pleased but again uncertain how to answer. What did they want from her? "I almost beat Peter at chess the other day."

"Did you? Good for you. He must have been careless, but you will beat him if you want to badly enough. Peter can see half a dozen moves ahead, but I don't believe he cares a fig about the game. It could take more time than it's worth to you, though."

"Maybe." Luc took the time, apparently. No mid-Cape rat could challenge him at chess. Chess and music, demanding skills, and scholarship and books.

They talked on awhile about literature and writing, and Sara felt very grown-up, as Luc always made her feel.

"Teatime, I think. A little early, but not too."

Inside the den, Lasa was working at the kitchen table, books and piles of manuscript around her. Luc's wife was nice, but different. Her knowledge of Greek and Latin was unusual even among rats. She seemed very serious, but Luc could make her laugh and often did. Sara liked her a lot and feared her just a little. Too smart, Grandfather said, though he didn't mean it. Too intense maybe. Perhaps what Sara really feared was wanting to be like Lasa and feeling unequal to the challenge. Lasa was pretty and slim and not always well, and Luc loved her.

"I've made scones. I don't think they're very good, but you might like some with your tea."

"I'd love some, Lasa." They wouldn't be as good as Luc's, but Sara would enjoy them anyway. Lasa's efforts at domesticity were spasmodic and endearing. She meant to play her part, even if her thoughts were caught up in Homeric hexameters. Luc really ran the household, with a cheerful competence that left Lasa little to fuss over.

They ate buttered scones and drank Lapsang souchong tea. Goodness knows where that had come from. The tangy taste of smoked Siberian pony hide? Sometimes hyperbole hit the mark.

And they talked. What rats do best, Sara thought: talk and eat. They talked about her studies, what all grown-ups asked about, in desperation, perhaps, and hope of some common ground or, as Luc said, genuine interest in her. Luc and Lasa were really interested, it seemed. Sara was learning French this year, from prim old Mademoiselle. She had a name, but she was known to three generations of adoring students as simply Miss. For how long and when the old rat had actually lived in Paris was unclear, but she recreated the experience convincingly for dozens of rat children who dreamed of romantic strolls along the Seine. Sara hoped someday to study Greek literature with Lasa, but not yet. She didn't dare to mention this.

And, surprisingly, they spoke of fish and fishing, and Sara was tempted to lay her burden on her aunt and uncle. It wasn't hers to share, however, for she had promised Peter not to tell. No, she had to carry it herself and make the best of it. In time one's pack could grow heavy with such worries, she supposed.

51

They waited until dusk to make their way across the fields to the Waterrats' hole. It was safer then. There were hugs and kisses when they arrived. None of them had seen much of Luc since the wedding. Lasa was shy in company but seemed content to listen. Someone had to listen, Sara thought, and she was glad to share the role.

Father and Peter and the clams were expected at any time. Grandfather tapped a keg, and they all had mugs of the new beer, Sara a small one, and John a mere thimbleful, a token really, but he was pleased to be included.

"It's awfully bitter, isn't it?" he whispered in Sara's ear.

"Yes," she whispered back. She couldn't see the reason for the fuss herself, but she knew Grandfather's brew was highly valued and his yeast sought after from surprisingly distant parts.

"Make way, make way." Voices came bellowing down the entrance tunnel, and Peter, Father, Tom, and old Henry himself struggled into the hall carrying heavy burlap bags of clacking shells.

"Should do us, I'd think," Tom said with satisfaction. Tom was big but very gentle and a polite and cheerful guest. He was always glad to lend his strength when a heavy stone or log needed to be moved, and, oddly, he was often sought as an arbitrator in the inevitable small disagreements of life.

"To the back kitchen, if you please." Mother pointed in the general direction of the big lower scullery, far down at the entrance to a rear tunnel. There much of the rough cooking was done, particularly in the warmer months. Fish was smoked there and maple syrup boiled down in the fall. There, too, was the pot big-enough-for-anything, as John called it, for lobster and for a clam feast such as they planned this night.

"Should make three batches," Tom offered.

"We can stuff ourselves," Peter agreed. "We'll have to add the shells to the Indian mounds and give the archaeologists a laugh."

"I imagine even archaeologists can tell the difference between thousand-year-old steamers and fresh ones."

"You'd think so, Tom, but they do have an amazing ability to see exactly what they want to see. They'll invent a theory and give it up only when they can't jam all the evidence into it, if then." Clamshells rattled into the steamer baskets.

"So I've noticed," Tom said, "and I often wonder why such a lunatic approach when they have perfectly good brains."

"It does seem crazy, but it could be one reason they make the discoveries, and we just adapt them. We have brains, too, but you don't move forward unless you're willing to make mistakes."

"Ah, well, let them," Tom said. "They can afford it better than we."

"Maybe," Peter agreed from under the great pot, where he was arranging charcoal briquettes, "but sometimes we pay for their mistakes."

"Um," Tom said, and Peter decided it was time to light the fire.

*   *   *

They ate in the kitchen, surrounded by gleaming pots and pans and rows of hanging ladles, spoons, knives, and cleavers. Usually dinner was a much more formal affair, with the family gathered around the big oak table in the dining room, but steamers were another matter. It was every rat for herself with clams, and they'd all end up awash in broth and butter.

"Mighty fine eating," Grandfather pronounced. He was the least disheveled of them, Sara noted, behind his vast white linen napkin. Decades of experience with steamed clams could make a difference. "We'll have old Henry and his family over one of these days. When we're having land food," he added with a chuckle.

"We'll do that, Dad," Mother agreed. "Maybe we can find a hen."

Sara saw Peter smile at that. You didn't just find fat roasters roaming wild, and though the thefts were blamed on skunks and foxes, there was always a risk involved. Where her elders' appetites were concerned, caution was sometimes outweighed, by necessity they'd say, though greed was far more like it. "Every rat his foolery," she'd heard Luc marvel, he who claimed that no one smelled his pipe.

The talk was mostly of food and family, as it usually was at table. It was a peaceful, pleasant accompaniment to feasting, Sara thought. She liked to hear about her aunts and countless cousins and their foibles. It made her feel safe and happy and a minor but important player in some never-ending epic of domesticity. Their own peculiarities made talk at other supper tables, she supposed. All possible, she'd come to see, through a common faith in the generosity of rats. No one, at any rate, would try to pin her down about her studies or her life amid the bowls of empty shells and puddles of clam juice.

"More beer, Dad?" Father was brandishing a half-empty pitcher like an auctioneer.

"No, I've had quite enough, thank you. Some coffee in a bit. I've still got to look in on old Helga. I need to talk with you first, though, Son."

"Sure thing." Father gave up on the pitcher and set it on the sink. Peter glanced at his father and grandfather. This was something new, Grandfather's recognition that Father had things to tell him about medicine.

Coffee and pecan pie, the perfect accompaniment to clams. Tom had insisted on bringing the pies. His mother had just made three, he said, and he would probably have eaten most of them. This way he was spared a few more pounds he didn't need.

"What are you and Peter up to, anyway?" Grandfather asked. "I've smelled solder several times this week."

"Radio, sir," Tom said. "We thought we'd learn a little about the technology."

"Like enough," Grandfather said dryly. "Take care messing about with the airwaves. We don't need any official curiosity. Have you finished the chemistry exercise I set you, Peter?"

"We'll be careful, Grandfather," Peter said, "and, no, not yet, but you said by the end of this week. Father needs to let me have the lab."

Father laughed. "You can have it tonight, then, Son. I don't feel so energetic after a feed like that."

Peter groaned.

"How's your pa, Tom?" Mother asked. Mother liked Tom. He stopped in to see her sometimes, and they'd talk history and old customs. The sort of thing Sara felt she'd heard once too often, but it was interesting to Tom, apparently.

"Much better, thanks. The pills did the trick, I guess. He's back pretty much to normal. He still rests a lot."

"No harm in that," Grandfather growled. "He's got a youngster with a strong back." And who could use the exercise, he might as well have added, but Tom just smiled. Peter knew Tom worked hard for his parents. It would take more than tunneling and carpentry to trim his extra pounds.

The pies vanished, and Tom had no more than his share. The coffee pot was empty finally, and Father and Grandfather went off together to discuss Grandfather's patient. Luc and Lasa had said little. Their happiness was complete and obvious, and it was a pleasure just to have them at the table. Luc was usually a great talker, and Sara loved to hear him tell of books and music and speculate on the world situation—the world of humans, that is. He hadn't come to talk tonight, he said, but he'd play a little if they'd like him to.

Their music was a shameless and nearly total borrowing from European classical traditions. There was music by Rattish composers, of course. It was interesting and favored the abilities and limitations of rats, but it was rarely adventurous. As with the other arts of life, rats were fine performers and sometimes brilliant in adaptation, but they lacked the demons that drove men to creativity.

Mother and Luc played for an hour, Bach and Brahms and the Franck Sonata in A for violin and piano, Mother's favorite. For all their constant chatter, the books and magazines and the millions of words they broadcast every day, the humans were barely comprehensible to rats. They poured their lives into building and tearing down again. They used their energies in pushing against one another and almost ignored the impersonal forces of famine and disease that truly harmed them. But in music they opened their hearts and minds in a way that rats could share. Sara watched Luc play, his fingers a blur on the strings and the bow alive, as if unguided by his paw. He became possessed at times, he said, an instrument of the music. And Luc was driven, really, more than any other rat she knew. In his publishing and in his playing he wanted to sow what he called the common achievements of civilization as widely as possible, almost as if there were a terrible need and too little time and not simply one day unfolding into another in the careful million-year history of their race.

"Bravo, Luc." Grandfather had returned from his call and sat deep in his own big chair, puffing on his calabash. Sara watched the smoke rise straight up in the still air of the den and hang like an obscure thought balloon above his head. Father might be the more brilliant one, Father and Peter like him, but Grandfather was the thinker. And yet he rarely shared his thoughts with anyone, not even her.

They talked on awhile, about more serious matters like new building in the woods and pesticides in French's Brook. Not the most cheery way to end an evening, Sara thought, and they'd reach no conclusions. Some problems were beyond consensus. She left them calmly discussing catastrophe and went back to *Moby Dick*, a more manageable disaster.

·9·

Tom poked a metal stake into the ground beside the knot.

"Mark," he called softly across the churchyard, and Peter began to reel in the two hundred feet of fishing line. Tom set up their homemade transit and hung the plumb bob directly over the little marker. Peter came up beside him as he tried to sight the weather vane through the guide tube. It wasn't easy even for a rat's eye, as the sky was overcast and the night was dark. He found it finally, a jaunty little schooner that had ridden out the winter storms on top of Saint Paul's steeple for four decades and in the daylight showed rather green about the hull.

"Twenty-two degrees." He calculated the side of the triangle in his head. "Eighty feet. You try it, Peter."

Peter looked. "Twenty-two degrees is right." No need to check Tom's math. "Do we have enough wire?"

"Better than a hundred and fifty feet in my pack. Plenty to take it through the drain to the rocks with some over, if the steeple is only eighty feet to the weather vane. I'd have said it was more.''

''Me, too. The tallest thing we've ever seen ought to be taller. High enough, though, surely? Nothing higher between here and North Cape except the bluffs over on the ocean side. Should make a beeline to Kendon's barn. Well . . . nothing left but to do it.''

''Right.'' Tom was not looking forward to this part of their plan. He was big and strong, but no climber ordinarily. He was just past the roly-poly stage and finally developing some hard muscle with this summer's digging. Something of his hesitation must have shown even in the darkness.

''You don't have to come, Tom. I can do it alone.''

''No.'' He shook his head. Where Peter went, he'd try to go. Peter and Tom had been friends as long as either one remembered. There were pictures of them in the sand together as no more than little balls of fur with glittery eyes. They'd lived in and out of each other's dens as much as their own and eaten at one another's tables and shared praises and rebukes from two sets of parents and grandparents. Later they'd explored every path and pond, and all the holes and gullies, tunnels, sinks, and sloughs within five miles in all directions. The mid-Cape was theirs as perhaps no others', not their preoccupied elders' or the single-minded marsh creatures', and certainly not the oblivious and neurotic humans' who rarely seemed to take an interest in anything beyond their own possessions.

Peter went first with the safety line, and Tom followed with the one hundred fifty feet of antenna wire in his pack. The climb up the long rainspout to the roof was easy, and the roof itself was safe though steep, but they used the rope for both. "No point to being a rat if you can't act like one," Tom had heard his grandpop say. He'd been afraid Peter would want to climb it cold to save the time. Maybe Peter understood his fear better than he showed. They worked their way up the spout, anchoring the line at every bracket. They left one nylon line at the edge of the roof and began another. Tom knew the theory of rock climbing. He'd read the books, but had climbed only a little. Peter knew his stuff, it seemed. That could be misleading, though. Peter read books, too, and he did everything so well the first time that you'd swear he was an expert. Someday Tom would follow him over one edge too far.

"Wait." Peter took the second rope straight up the roofline to the corner of the steeple, stopping every four feet to wedge a clip beneath the slates. There were easy handholds around the steeple base and a flat area just where the roof peak joined it and where they could stop and reconnoiter. The wind was stronger here, or perhaps it had risen as they climbed.

"So that's the easy part done," Peter said. "Maybe you should wait here. I'll take it slow and careful and drive in spikes, but it is straight up the clapboards. You can feed me the antenna wire as I go. No need for us both to make the climb." Tom didn't answer right away. "It would be safer for me to go alone," Peter continued, as if reluctantly.

"All right," Tom said. Safer for both of us, he thought regretfully. Oh well, we all have our talents. He stretched out on the shelf and watched the ocean breakers half a mile to the east. He'd never seen them quite like this. It was like the view from an airplane, he supposed, though he'd never flown and never expected to. The whitecaps shone even in the darkness, and the beach was faintly luminescent. The land below was black, dotted with ten thousand points of light, the cottages that disappeared beneath the trees by day. Tom didn't watch Peter's progress. There was nothing he could do to help, so better not to think about it.

"I'm up." Peter's voice was faint above the howling wind. Quick work, unless Tom had lost track of time. No, only five minutes by the luminous screen of his watch. Peter was much faster without him. Well, he hadn't watched. The antenna wire had stopped uncoiling. Peter had tied it around the base of the weather vane and let another ten feet trail down the dark cone of the roof. He was finished now, but not yet coming down. He was climbing up, in fact.

"Peter?"

"I just want to reach the top. No point in going this far and . . ." But Tom could barely hear him.

"No point in going farther, Peter. Let it be," he shouted. But Peter was almost there. He was at the mast of the little ship, and then he stood, stretched on tiptoe for a second only, higher than the little crow's nest, the highest thing that moment on the Middle Cape. And then a blast of wind tore him off the mast and left him dangling from the point of the big brass arrow, his feet clawing the air and his tail thrashing wildly. For a moment Tom thought Peter was gone, but he hung on, whipped and buffeted, swinging erratically in the storm. It had begun to rain, and Tom heard distant thunder. He hesitated only an instant and then began to climb.

61

It was hard, much harder than anything he'd ever done before. He knew that if it weren't for Peter, he would give it up as impossible. There were cracks and projecting shingles along the edge of the steeple, and there was Peter's rope, but half the time he dangled from one paw while searching for another hold. It was like doing fifty, a hundred, one-armed pull-ups. He made the steeple roof with only a little strength to spare and hitched his way up to the point. He hoped Peter had anchored the rope well. The wind helped now, as it plastered him against the shingles and seemed to boost him toward the weather vane.

"Coming," he shouted. He was afraid Peter hadn't seen him and might let go in despair. Peter didn't answer. Tom grasped the base of the brass rod that held the vane, just as a thunderclap cracked the sky above them and a flash of jagged lightning showed Peter hanging on. Tom wrapped his tail around the rod and stretched his long body out toward Peter. It took a moment before they could trust their hold, and then Tom drew him in toward the shaft, slowly, pulling with his legs and tail.

"Got it." Peter's voice was like a stranger's. "Thanks, Tom." They hung there a moment.

"You okay?"

"Okay."

Tom started slowly down, and Peter followed. The storm roared around them, but they were in little danger now. The line would hold. There was no thought of trying to recover it. It could stay there, a small mystery for some steeplejack. They rested on the platform at the steeple's base.

"Tom, I'm sorry. That was the bravest thing I've ever seen."

Tom just shook his head. "Let's forget it."

The climb down from the base of the steeple was easy now. Tom went first, and Peter collected the line and clips as he followed. The wind had dropped as well, and they were sheltered by the grove of full-grown pines behind the church.

"Well, it's up," Tom said, when they once more stood on the sandy ground beside the stone foundation of the old church. "Shall we get the wire?" They'd dropped the coil down the corner rain spout.

"Sure," Peter agreed.

"You do want to try to call tomorrow night?"

"Yes, sure. We said we would." He was being ridiculous, he felt. It was all his idea, and Tom, on top of having saved his life, was trying to cheer him on.

"Sorry, Tom. I do. It's just reaction, and guilt. Let's do it." He set off across the grass, and Tom followed, his arms and legs still trembling just a little, but with a half smile on his long muzzle. Water was still pouring from the drainpipe, but Peter had no trouble splashing his way up the thirty feet of gentle slope to where the coil lay at the bottom of the spout. There was a handy crack just where the last pipe emerged from the ground to spill the runoff into a little creek. They threaded the wire beneath the stones and into the small dry cave within the gully's low retaining wall.

"Tomorrow after supper then?"

"Right," Peter agreed. "Be careful crossing the swamp." Tom laughed. Peter was all right.

But not unmarked, apparently. "Are you okay?" John asked when Peter appeared in the living room.

63

"I'm fine," Peter said breezily. "Just tired. I think I'll go read a little. Good night."

"Harrummph"—Grandmother's all purpose comment on the mysterious insufficiencies of the young. Harrummph indeed, thought Sara. What was that about?

·10·

Peter felt much better in the morning, but nothing could take away the memory of his foolishness or of Tom's courage. The debt would be there always, a humbling thought. It was a lesson, too, and not a cheap one, though they'd had the price, just barely. Your life wasn't entirely yours to spend. So he'd been told, of course, but some things you had to find out for yourself.

He kept to his room and studied, with a lot of application but less success, he felt. He joined the others at lunch and wasn't particularly good company. No one seemed to notice, and he finally had to laugh at himself. He was out of joint and concealing it too well. But what could he complain about? His life was just the way it was supposed to be. He spent part of the afternoon scrubbing the lower kitchen and then swam furiously in the bathing pool for nearly an hour.

Luc came alone to supper and talked. His wife was spending a few days with her sister in South Bay. He was the old Luc and the new at once, quite an overpowering combination. He talked of books and music and politics and plain gossip, and in everything he talked of Lasa, though he rarely spoke her name. Peter had to say very little and enjoyed himself.

Tom arrived in time for dessert and coffee and afterward settled down in Peter's reading chair. Peter closed his notebook and reshelved the texts he'd been working with. It was dark already, Peter knew. Like any other rat he was aware, from hardly noticed clues, of time and weather and the quality of dark and light in the fields above.

"No point in going yet?"

"Nope."

Peter took out his guitar and ran through his small repertoire of classical pieces, simple arrangements of Carulli, Sor, and Bach. It was one of the few things he had no special talent for, so he obstinately persisted in it. It didn't bother Tom, who'd heard it all many times before. He found one of Peter's old Tarzan novels and read three chapters.

"Peter?"

"Hmm?"

"Why are we doing this?"

Peter just looked at Tom a moment. "Because you shamed me into going on with it after last night. But I don't suppose that's what you mean?"

Tom shook his head.

"I don't know. It's not that I don't have enough to do." He waved at the row of books on the wall above his desk. "It was Kendon's idea, but it sounded good to me. I don't know, Tom. I'm just fidgety sometimes. I'm buried in all

66

these books, and I feel like I've never had a . . . a real adventure, I guess.'' It sounded idiotic.

Tom laughed and held up *Tarzan and the Jewels of Opar*.

''Well, hardly,'' Peter smiled, too. ''So it's dumb. It's wrong. It's taking unnecessary risks and messing with technology we don't even need. Don't you ever feel restlessness? Wanderlust?''

''No, to be honest,'' Tom said, ''but I feel discouraged sometimes; not often. I wouldn't mind being buried in books.''

''Then why don't—'' Peter stopped when Tom raised his paw. ''Isn't it better to talk about it?''

''I don't think so,'' Tom said with finality. ''Sorry I brought it up.''

They glared at each other for a moment, and then Peter snickered, and Tom smiled sheepishly.

''Ready to go?''

''Sure.''

They sauntered through the den and up the tunnel, the radio in Peter's shoulder bag. Only Sara, at the big table where she often studied, saw them go. She would have liked to follow, but she knew her limits and merely sighed.

Tom lit a candle in the small rock cave. The antenna was attached, and the dial of the transmitter glowed dimly. At the beep of Peter's watch, checked earlier with the Cape news-and-weather station, he flipped the sending switch and spoke into the microphone. ''Peter calling Kendon.'' They'd picked a frequency that was usually clear. Human listeners would hear no voices to stir their curiosity; rat speech ordinarily ranged far above what they could detect.

The sounds might be recorded, though, and could be recognized by a computer as some form of communication, and would probably give the cryptographers fits for years to come. The risk seemed slight to Peter.

The speaker crackled for a moment, and then they heard Peter's cousin's familiar voice. "Kendon calling Peter. Nicely done. I have a message for your father. Over."

"Peter to Kendon, go on. Over." Peter looked at Tom, who just made a face. This was an unexpected development and not a particularly welcome one.

"Most of our insulin was destroyed in a fire. There's none nearer than your supply. By sharing we have enough for a week. Your great-aunt Ruth may be in a bad way. Can your father send some? Over."

"Peter to Kendon, will do. I'll bring it myself. Over."

"Great. It'll be good to see you. We'll have a dune party. What's new down your way? Over."

They talked on for a few minutes until Peter began to feel nervous. Grandfather's warning about the airwaves was in his mind.

"See you soon. Over and out." It felt to him a little like a chapter in *The Radio Boys Go on the Air*. He looked at Tom. "So."

"So, indeed. It seems we'll have to share our experiment with your father."

"Guess so. Come with me?"

"Sure."

They packed the radio away and returned to the Waterrats' den. Sara was still working at the big table and looked up in surprise when Tom and Peter reappeared so soon. Something was wrong, she could tell—different, anyway.

"Where's Father?"

"In the lab. What's up?"

Peter hesitated only a moment. "We talked with Kendon on the radio. They need insulin."

In the end they had to tell the story to everyone.

"How did you manage to reach North Cape?" Father asked.

"We ran an antenna up the steeple at Saint Paul's," Peter answered resignedly.

"Huh. A little risky, wasn't it?"

"Yes, sir," Peter said. "It was a mistake, in fact."

"And a lesson, I gather?"

"Yes, sir. A cheaper one than I deserved. But . . ."

"But it did us all a good turn, eh? All right, Son. Remember, you get only so many free lessons."

Peter nodded. That was done. "I said I'd bring the insulin. I was pretty sure we had it. Can I, Father?"

"I don't see why not. You might as well finish what you've started. Yes, we have plenty." There were only about a dozen cases of diabetes at Cape End, Peter remembered. Human insulin would do them no good, of course. The rodent product was made in Bayport, a hundred miles away, but there were supplies here and at several places on the upper Cape.

"You shouldn't go alone."

"I'll go with him. I'm sure my folks will feel I ought to."

"All right, Tom. You'd best go ask them now. You'll need to leave tomorrow evening."

"Can I go, too?" Sara couldn't believe her boldness, and then she had a sudden horror that Peter might feel blackmailed because of the raccoons. "I don't *have* to come, Peter." She stressed the word and even shook her head.

Peter smiled. "I'd like it if you could." He'd understood her. He looked at his parents. There was a silence.

"Sara might find good use for a trip like this." It was Luc who spoke.

"Well . . . What do you think, Ed?" Mother didn't sound upset.

Thank goodness for her uncle. Sara felt her heart soar. Father wouldn't like it, but he'd go along with Mother on something like this, and Mother trusted Luc. Fortunately Grandfather had gone to bed.

"I guess so." Father obviously didn't like it, but he wouldn't stop her. A trip down-Cape, with Tom and Peter, hiking and camping on the beach. She tried to look calm. Rats didn't run around and shout for joy, but sometimes they wanted to. "A good use for a trip like this." What did Luc mean?

Tom went home and was back in half an hour. He could go. If his parents had any misgivings, he didn't say. It wasn't a particularly difficult or dangerous journey, but none of them had ever been so far without their parents, and it wasn't just a pleasure trip. Getting the insulin to North Cape was a heavy responsibility. If somehow they failed in the task, it could mean the suffering and death of fellow rats.

They talked a bit about their preparations, but it was getting late. They could get a good night's sleep and spend the day planning and packing. They wouldn't start until after dark.

·11·

Sara woke to the smell of coffee and a confused feeling that something good was about to happen. It took her a moment to remember the events of the night before and the impending trip. She was going with Peter and Tom to North Cape. It would take at least three days to get there, and she would see sights she'd never seen before, have new experiences, and visit relatives, some of whom were for her still only amusing characters in dinner-table tales. A real adventure. She lay on the comfortable dried-grass mattress in the corner of her neat, whitewashed room and thought these pleasant thoughts until the aroma of bacon was added to that of coffee. Breakfast was proceeding without her. She washed quickly and joined her brothers in the kitchen.

"Morning."

"Morning." The usually ebullient little John looked downcast. Evidently he had heard about the trip. It made her feel sad briefly. She didn't like causing anyone discomfort, and it was a fairly new experience for her. She'd noticed only this year that she could make her parents and her friends genuinely unhappy without meaning to. And last month she'd felt the way that John did now, when Peter got to go with Uncle Alfred on his boat. It was just a gentle sail along the bay, no deep-sea lobster hunt, but all her grandfather's headshaking made no difference. She had wanted to go along. It didn't seem fair to have to trade envy now for guilt. Well, she'd try to be extra nice to John, and she wouldn't let it get her down. You had to go on, carrying your feelings with you or chucking them by the road, whatever seemed right at the time. John's face brightened suddenly as a large plate of apple-and-walnut waffles with blueberry syrup was put down in front of him. Some ailments were easily treated.

". . . plans after lunch," Peter was saying. Tom would come over, and they'd make their preparations then and nap for a few hours before supper. Rats operated in the dark or light, whichever best suited their situation, and ratnapped when they could. Long trips through unfamiliar territory were best begun at night. A small price to pay for being a rat, it was said. Sara wondered sometimes, though. Their glimpses of day's beauty were few and fleeting. There didn't seem to be a choice, however.

Lunch was leftovers, a peculiar mixture of warmed-up stir-fry concoctions and watercress sandwiches. The talk was of the trip. Father and Grandfather debated the merits of the bay and ocean routes and came to no conclusion. Their goal was speed and safety, though, and Peter's seemed to be to squeeze the maximum of interest from the expedition.

"This is a serious business, Peter, a rescue operation.

That should come first. Save your side trips for the journey home, if you still have the energy.''

"Yes, sir," Peter said. "We will. What I thought, though, was that starting straight up the ocean beach would be safe and fast. At Buffum's Hollow, we can cut east across the Cape to the bay side, make time north along the flats at low tide, and then go back over to the ocean below High Light, for the long trip around the dune beaches.''

"Hmm," Father said, "a little complicated, but it should do. You won't find much cover on the beach up north, less than here. Fewer humans, too, but you've got to stop early, and remember, plan an escape route. Just cover isn't enough.''

"Yes, Father," Peter said, with admirable restraint, Sara thought. Even she knew all this. It was like a good-luck charm, really. They were always telling you to be careful, as if that would keep you safe. It seemed a waste of breath. Luc would laugh, though, and tell her to be generous, that grown-ups couldn't help this sort of thing.

Tom came shortly after lunch, and they all went into the dining room and spread the section maps out on the table. These were the big topographic survey maps, liberated long ago from some official trash bin. They were thirty years out of date, but fortunately most of the lower Cape was a government preserve, the Rat Conservancy Project Luc had called it once, and it had surely been a blessing for them. Little had changed on the National Shorelands except through the constant action of the wind and sea, playing havoc with the little brown contour lines along the coast. The sand roads, ponds and streams, and rare outbuildings were still where the map had put them, and little had been added. The railroad was shut down, to the sorrow of old-timers who had liked its roar and whistle, but its roadbed remained as a bike and hiking trail and was often the shortest nighttime distance between two points, if you didn't mind the asphalt beneath your paws.

Sara memorized their route in full detail. She had a mind for this, even beyond the usual capability of rats to remember an astounding welter of detail. How did humans accomplish so much, she wondered, with minds apparently like sieves?

There was more debate about packing food. Tom had notions of grand picnics on the beach. Father's solution was dehydrated rations and fresh water. They compromised, of course. Tom would cook the next day's dinner, and thereafter they'd eat light and travel fast. Each of them would carry a small vacuum container of insulin. (These had been designed with this sort of transportation in mind. Many of the rats' important supplies were carried long distances, along with the food and other necessities of the bearer. It made for efficiency and thinking most things through ahead of time. Waste was rarely a possibility for them, much less a failing.)

They would bring their books, a textbook and a reading book for each of them. There was no rule that said so. It was just the inexorable logic of rodent minds, Sara concluded. Even Peter, her so-often-unpredictable brother, was bringing his calculus text and Thoreau's *Walden*, Mother's recommendation, he said. Tom carried a thick and heavy-looking volume, a history of the Middle Ages in Europe, the nonrodent view. He was big and strong enough to carry it at least, along with the ingredients for their barbecue. She couldn't see what else he had in his large pack. She would bring her French book and *Moby*

Dick. She was halfway through now and caught by its fascination. What better book to bring on a journey by the sullen sea? And her little journal, of course, her gift from Luc. She would write her first brief entry this afternoon before they started. That was all, really. A pencil and two pens, her pocketknife, which she must sharpen, come to think of it, and her share of the food and pots and pans, whatever Tom had in mind. She'd carry it all with pleasure, though the vacuum cylinder was more substantial than she'd expected. It was remarkable how heavy the absence of something could turn out to be.

Tom came back for supper at the Waterrats'. Mother had clearly gone some lengths to make their last meal, as Peter insisted on calling it, a very good one. A roasting hen appeared magically, and old Henry missed out on this one. It was served stuffed with apricots and garlic, a combination that acted like catnip on rat appetites. There was fresh corn on the cob as well, the first of the season from French's garden. They were careful not to take too much.

All in all, it was a glorious feast, and they were sorry only that they couldn't eat until they were stuffed. They had a long way to go that night and would start as soon as it was well dark.

"If we never get another bite for the whole week, that should hold us," Tom said.

"I seriously doubt that, Tom," Father said dryly, "but you'll manage, I'm sure. You're very resourceful along those lines, I've noticed."

"Yes, sir," Tom said a bit uncertainly, and Grandfather laughed.

"Don't let them get to you, Tom. Successful foraging

is a good old-fashioned virtue we see too little of these days.''

"Coffee, Dad?'' Mother was coming to Tom's rescue, Sara was pleased to see. ''You might as well have some, too, Sara. It's going to be a long night.''

"Yes, please, Mother.'' It was at that. She'd never spent a whole night traveling, a daunting thought. She hoped she could keep up. Doubts attacked her suddenly. She was faster than any rat she knew except Peter and Uncle Luc. She could run rings around poor Tom. But all night? She'd go until she dropped, but she hoped it wouldn't come to that. A humiliating thought.

"Ready?''

"Yes, ready.'' Right. As ready as she'd ever be.

They said good-bye. It would have seemed an unemotional parting to anyone who knew nothing of rats and of the deep feelings of family and solidarity that enveloped their lives. Sara felt a little frightened and not nearly as pleased to be leaving as she'd expected to. It would pass. It had better. She shouldered her not-so-light pack and, with a last look at her family, turned and followed Peter up the tunnel.

Outside in the field it was an ordinary summer night, no more sinister or dramatic than the night a week ago when she'd followed Peter to his rendezvous with the raccoons. Her emotions settled, and her spirits rose as they walked three abreast along the open footpath beneath a moonless but starry sky and talked of ordinary things. She was simply one of them, she was glad to notice, not a younger sister or, worse, the little sister of a friend. They took the paved road around Salt Pond, something they might not have done in unfamiliar territory. Here they knew the traffic and the turns and a hundred hiding places, and they saved themselves a good hour of difficult travel through the brush.

They stayed on the road past the Coast Guard station and along the top of the last ocean dune to the lighthouse. From here they would follow the ocean beach itself as far as Buffum's Hollow, where they'd find shelter for the day.

Yellow light shone from windows in both the station and the keeper's house, and shadows moved in the rooms beyond. How strange it would seem to announce your presence to the world so boldly, to live in the sun on the top of a cliff and beneath a great beacon at night and have no fear. The humans were afraid of the dark, of course. They knew little of the beauty of the night. With their poor senses, weakened in only a few thousand years by too great a dependence on other abilities, it must seem to them a veil or blindness rather than a revelation of all that sunlight hid. They'd meet no humans on the dune.

And what a sight the humans would miss. It was a good clear night, and beach and cliff and water magnified the starlight so that stones and drift logs and the rats themselves cast faint shadows on the sand. A light sea breeze did no more than cool their fur, and the breakers crumpled and hissed toward their feet with satisfying regularity. They talked less now and went more quickly. It was pleasant, easy, almost hypnotizing as their feet seemed barely to touch the sand. They were moving shadows on the broad white beach, but Sara felt no fear. If any other conscious-ness were aware of them, it seemed somehow benevolent. Only from the dark sea beyond the line of surf did she sense a hidden and perhaps mindless menace.

They reached Buffum's Hollow early and considered

going on, but dawn would find them before they came to the next break in the sea cliff, and there would be a danger then of encountering surf casters on the beach, those rather spiritual few who seemed to use fishing as an excuse to stand in the breakers and stare out to sea for hours. They might let the rats pass without notice, but then again, they might not.

A splendid structure of drift logs and lumber jutted from the dune not far up the hollow, and there Peter wished them to stay. It was certainly a boldly public hideaway, but there was a short tunnel connecting with the grass and brush beyond. Father wouldn't approve, but Father had no say in this, and whatever Sara's misgivings, she'd make no objections, either. She rather liked it here, in fact. She found a comfortable wood surface just inside the overhanging logs and stretched at length, her nose facing the sea. The breeze had stiffened, and a morning mist began to form. The air was soft and moist and sweet as it ruffled her fur. This was splendid, her favorite kind of weather. She would read a little before she slept, but just now she was content to watch the waves pile one on another on the shore below. The feeling of menace had faded, too, and only a sense of vast wilderness remained, a wildness that was the source of all energy and freedom, for her and everything.

She woke to the smell of coffee. It was probably a conditioned reflex that would wake her anywhere at any time. Good old Tom had contrived to make a feast for them here in their grandstand overlooking Buffum's Beach. Boiled coffee, bacon, scrambled eggs, and even toast, a little scorched in spots, but heavenly. There were fishermen in the surf, but only a few. The day had turned cloudy and raw, a break for rats. They could start traveling again late in the afternoon.

Something moved at the corner of her vision. She turned her head and stiffened in sudden fear. A dog, up the hollow a hundred yards and coming their way. It was with one of the fishermen or on its own, exploring from the houses they knew to be back in the trees. It was a big generic hound, with black lips and a lolling tongue, a comic horror. Peter saw it, too, and appeared unmoved. The dog meandered down the path, sniffing at rocks and bushes and stopping once to lift its leg on a weathered piling. Sara held her breath as it veered their way in its foolish sideways canine trot. It paused and wrinkled its nose in distaste, then trotted on and sat beside a tackle box and wagged its tail in immense self-satisfaction. Ignorance was bliss, presumably.

"I spread a package of scent," Peter said. "I doubt we'll see much more activity today if this weather holds. It's getting nice and nasty."

"Ah," was all she could think to say. She might have known. Her pulse returned to normal, and she poured herself another cup of coffee.

The coffee tasted wonderful in the mist. Everything did, as always along the water.

"Thanks for letting me come, both of you."

Peter looked surprised, as if it hadn't actually been partly his decision. "Well, glad to have you." Tom just smiled. "I'm sorry they've had this emergency at North Cape," Peter continued, "but as long as they were going to have it anyway, I'm just glad we have the excuse for the trip. I wish we didn't need another reason for an expedition like this.''

''You know what your grandfather would say to that,'' Tom said. ''I guess I agree with you, though. Books are fine, but I'd like to see more firsthand.''

''Me, too,'' said Sara. ''Like the three little pigs who went out to seek their fortune,'' she added with a grin.

''Is that what we're doing?'' Tom said. He almost seemed to expect an answer.

''Maybe so,'' said Peter.

They cleaned their breakfast things and talked a little more. Sara worked through two chapters in her French grammar, doing the exercises in her head, and fell asleep again. Peter gently closed her book and stuck it in her pack. The first watch was his, and he worked on calculus awhile, glancing up frequently at the scene below. The fishermen left in a group, hungry for their own breakfasts probably, and the dog went with them. The day turned darker, and the breeze became a stiff sea wind, bringing strange aquatic smells from lord knew where, perhaps the distant African shores. Tom spelled him, and Peter slept. Sara had the last watch before it would be time to fix their supper, and she read in *Moby Dick*. Peter woke by himself in the late afternoon and watched his sister silently with some amusement. Ahab himself might have stalked through their camp without raising the alarm.

·12·

". . . with four cloves of garlic and just a touch of cara-
way."

"More than a touch, I'd have said, but it's delicious,
Tom. The best beach stew ever." Peter helped himself to
a second bowlful as Tom smiled benignly at the honest
praise.

"It's terrific," Sara agreed. It was. Tom had planned
their picnic carefully. There was a loaf of rich, dark bread
as well. One of his mother's specialties. Crusty, nourish-
ing, and chewy, a highly virtuous food, as Peter said, and
tasty too. Healthy food, the humans would call it with their
maddeningly inconsistent use of language. Why did she
think of them again? She rarely did.

The rain had held off, but the wind had grown stronger
over the course of the day, and the temperature had dropped
rapidly with darkness.

"We'd just be plowing into a gale all night," Peter said.

"I vote we cut across to the bay now, at least until the weather changes."

"No argument from me," Tom said.

"Fine," Sara agreed. She hadn't looked forward all that much herself to hours of battling the damp, cold breeze. The bay shore here was unknown territory to her, as unknown as the familiar Cape could be. They packed their few belongings and advanced cautiously up the hollow. The sand trail changed into a narrow and broken macadam road, and old wooden houses appeared among the stunted oaks.

"There!" Sara almost tripped over Peter's tail as he stopped suddenly and pointed toward an old house with a sagging porch and little square windows beneath the peak of its roof. "Thoreau and Channing spent the night in that house in 1850 and talked with an old oysterman who could remember hearing the cannon fire at Bunker Hill across the bay. It was in his book about the Cape."

"Goodness," Tom was impressed but cautious. "That would make him . . . well, in his nineties at least. And fifty miles across the water, if it were true."

"They believed him, anyway. Some things you just like to believe whether they're true or not."

Tom nodded. "The bane of the historian."

A door opened, and they ducked into the shadows as light spilled out on the road and was followed by a tangle of small and larger children who immediately set off inland along the road.

"I guess we follow," Peter said.

The children moved at a good pace and slowed the rats only a little. They clearly had a destination in mind, the movies probably. There were a few more houses on the road but no more humans about, or dogs, a bigger worry. Then there was light ahead, an extraordinary amount of light, it seemed to Peter, a little north of where the town lay, he thought.

"Do you remember the map, Sara? What are we looking at?"

"A ball field?" Sara remembered it. There had been nothing about lights, of course.

"Baseball?" There was an odd note of pleasure in Tom's voice, almost of reverence.

"It's a good bet it isn't hockey in July."

"Could we . . . have a look, Peter?"

"Now who's indulging a whim?" Peter was amused. "It's okay with me. Sara?"

"Sure." She wasn't going to object, not to this, anyway.

"Not long," Tom said.

They approached the glow in the sky, slipping off the road as a few cars passed them. There were other hikers as well, and they had to dawdle at times, but they were traveling generally west toward the bay, at least. The ball field was an old one, with wooden bleachers and a simple wire fence. They had only to climb an ancient maple to have as good a view as the other spectators—better, really. The tree was at the edge of a small woodland park, so there was little danger of their being trapped. It was unusual, though, for them to be so near this many humans, and Sara felt nervous.

There was a long series of semi-incoherent announcements on a loudspeaker—perhaps the humans never listened to one another, anyway—and then a wavery recording of "The Star-Spangled Banner," the one national song that few of them could sing at all, Luc had cheerfully pointed out. Humans were such endearing idiots at times that it seemed tragic they represented so much danger, even to themselves.

They watched three innings. It was pretty interesting, Sara thought. The players demonstrated an amazing grace at times, leaping and diving after the ball and making long and accurate throws in almost the same motion. They hadn't entirely lost touch with their limbs, it seemed, despite their ordinarily bumbling ways and the pervasive machinery of their daily lives. A long drive flashed over the fence quite near them. "A grand slam!" Tom cried, nearly falling off the branch in his excitement, and they had to draw back into the shadows as a horde of little boys came scrambling after the ball. It was Tom who finally suggested that they go on. It was his responsibility, really, and he accepted it. Sara would have stayed still longer.

"Thank you. That was splendid," Tom said wistfully.

"Thank you too," Peter said. "I thoroughly enjoyed it. Sometimes it really is the master civilization, isn't it?"

"Uh-huh." Tom's grunted agreement evidently accompanied his own thoughts on the matter. "It may be that they simply have more freedom to play than we do. If we could turn night into day when we chose to, we might accomplish more as well."

"Maybe. They got baseball right. I wish we could try it."

"No kidding. Why not, Peter, on the beach some moonlit night? The Putterman crowd would go for it."

"And the old folks would have a fit. Some human would

spot us, and we'd end up in the *National Investigator* next to the two-headed Martians.''

Tom laughed softly. "So, who'd believe it?"

Every rat his foolery, Sara thought to herself. Luc was right. What was hers, she wondered?

They cut northwest across the narrow neck of the peninsula. It widened further north, and they'd have to keep to the bay shore now until it narrowed once again and took its final westward swing toward North Cape. The countryside was strange to them, and yet familiar. The same old elms and maples lined the roads close in to town. Groves of graceful locust trees soared over soft lawn grasses and fragrant flower gardens, and then near the shore the pitch-pine forest took over once again. It was an older forest here, trees sixty to seventy feet in height, planted in the previous century and outgrown their usefulness as fuel and lumber. Their value now was beauty, a utility unguessed by those who set out these gawky pines a century ago.

They followed what trails they found, the haunts of possums, raccoons, and other rats. The night was dark, though not entirely black. Here and there a star shone through thin clouds. The wind was slowed by trees, and the temperature rose steadily, still cool and comfortable for traveling. A smell of skunk masked every other scent for half a mile, a time to be alert, though really only the worst fool of a dog would be at large this late, and together they were a match for any cat or fox. No one troubled them, however, and they came by midnight to the bay.

The tide was just two hours out, which was no surprise to them and much less than simple luck. The tide had been in their calculations from the start. Otherwise they might have continued up the ocean side. This way they'd have a good three hours along the mile-wide flats. On a night like this, a quarter mile from shore, the world was theirs. They would be invisible to the unlikely nocturnal stroller and their light scent would be overwhelmed by the rich smell of salt and sea. No owl would hunt out here, Peter reasoned. The owls' information about rats was a whole geologic age behind. Like the humans, the rats had caught the fast track of their conscious minds and leaped past evolution. They had no less need of food and shelter, in terms of their individual lives, but as a race they, too, had gone beyond zoology to sail uncertainly among the stars.

They cut across the flats toward their still-distant goal. They'd be driven back to land eventually by the returning tide, but now they could make time. They loped awhile until Tom begged for mercy. He could march a million miles, he said, but if they insisted on a race, they'd have to go without him. Sara could have run much farther, but even she would flag before her brother. She was secretly grateful to Tom for sparing her this small humiliation. They walked again and talked more peacefully. The flats did that to you, she had noticed before. They brought out the philosopher that was just beneath the practical hide of every rat. It was their equivalent of walking in the sun, she supposed, of freedom and individuality. You were as big almost as the sands about you and the sky above, and your thoughts refused to stick on points of grammar or leaky faucets. You were also not alone and very much aware of this. Old Mother Westwind or whoever—he or she or it—was there.

"Maybe it's that we've just not had our turn," Tom

said. He was still meditating on Peter's comment that humans had the master civilization. "We haven't had our innings yet. And it won't come in our lifetime."

"It won't come until they've struck out?" said Peter a little grimly.

"Well, maybe."

"And maybe when they do, the game is over, or it gets called on account of darkness. Or maybe we already had our chance and blew it, Tom."

"So we should put our oar in now, you're saying?" Tom asked.

"It's always a possibility."

"No, it's not," Tom said with finality.

They walked on in silence. No one asked Sara to break the tie.

Lulled by the wind in her fur and the soft scrunch of wet sand beneath her paws, Sara's thoughts roamed aimlessly from past to present and out among the patterns printed on the sand by wave and current, endlessly repeating first one rippling texture, then another and another, branching and converging and tailing out and starting once again, with patterns within patterns, the small amusements of vast forces or of an all-engulfing mind.

They turned back toward the beach well before the first hint of dawn showed above the pines. They needed time to cross the narrowed neck of the westward-curling Cape and find a daylight lair on the National Shorelands that was comfortable and safe. The dune-side beach was farther around, but the only way for them. The bay beach was peopled, unlike the ocean shore.

"Psst." Peter's warning stopped her instantly, and she stood rock still, straining eyes and ears. Her senses were the best of any of theirs, and she could hear it now, a strange rasping sound, breathing almost certainly, but not normal breathing. The scent of human was in the air as well. They could cut farther up the flats to come ashore. But Peter wasn't moving.

"It's someone sick or injured." He spoke softly. "I'm going to see."

"No," she was about to say, but he was gone. She and Tom followed cautiously, reluctantly, and allied in disapproval. The sounds grew louder, and she saw what she expected to, a human, a full-grown man, lying on his back unconscious and breathing with great difficulty. Peter was at his head.

"Come back, Peter," Tom said. It was obvious there was no danger of the man's hearing them. "You don't know what he has."

Peter reached out his paw and touched the man's temple. Sara shivered inwardly. "Heart attack, most likely," Peter said. "The pulse is fast and irregular. He'll probably die if he doesn't get help."

"So?" Tom said.

"So," Peter said. "You saved my life, Tom. Why can't I save his?"

This was all mysterious to Sara. Tom saved Peter's life? And what was the connection?

"You know why," Tom said. He wasn't angry or upset, just very calm and reasonable.

"I know why, Tom. But I'm going to do it anyway, and that I don't understand. You can stay out of it. You should, both of you. I don't know what I'll do. Just . . . get help somehow."

88

No one spoke for a moment, and then Tom said, "Not alone."

Sara found her voice. "What can we do, Peter?"

"I don't know. Find a house. Raise a fuss and get someone down here."

"That'll be easy enough," Tom said. "We'll just knock on a door. That should produce a fuss, and bring them here as well, if we happen to run this way for our lives."

"Something like that," Peter admitted. "We don't have time for anything very fancy. He doesn't, either. No need to take more chances than necessary, though. Let's find a house."

"Peter." Peter looked at Sara with a kind of desperate patience. "Couldn't we take something of his, so they'd understand what it was about?"

"Yes, of course. That's a very good idea." He smiled at her. "Thank you." She didn't think he was thanking her just for the idea, somehow.

Unfortunately the man hadn't been carrying anything— no convenient hat or walking stick. He had probably just been getting some exercise.

"His wallet. I can feel it. We'll have to turn him over. Just a little. Help me push."

She'd never had to do anything so distasteful in her life. She tried to ignore the smell and the unpleasant spongy feel of his body beneath the shirt and pushed with all her might. He wasn't a giant, fortunately, and together they were strong enough to roll him onto his side. Peter nipped the button from his pocket, and when that failed to dislodge the wallet, simply bit and ripped the cloth.

There were houses on the low bluff that overlooked the

beach. Most of them were dark, but a light showed in one. The man's house, maybe.

They gathered at the door. Like trick-or-treaters, thought Sara wildly. Such clever little costumes.

"The glass," Peter said. "In case of emergency, break glass." He sounded on edge himself. "Help me find a stone."

Tom found something better than a stone: a four-foot piece of metal pipe, just lying by the drive. They shouldered it like a battering ram and on Peter's count drove it into the door with a splintering crash. They'd left the wallet lying open in the center of the porch.

They just had time to reach the shadows when a woman appeared in the doorway. Thank goodness, Peter thought. His one fear was that the man had been alone. The woman saw the wallet, all right. She picked it up. More lights came on, and someone ran to the next cottage. The humans were mystified, of course, but the alarm had been raised, at least. Sara froze as a powerful flashlight swept over them and then returned and pinned them to the sand. There was shouting, and they turned and ran. It wasn't really in their plan to lead the rescuers to the man, but as long as they had to run anyway. . . . She went ahead. Peter came last—no arguing with him on this. It was his responsibility. Lights and voices followed them. They passed the man, still on his side and still breathing, though they didn't stop to see. More shouts. They had found him. Lights spilled across the beach around them.

"Damn," Peter said. "Why can't they tend to first things first?"

"They're scared and angry and looking for something

to blame," Tom said, breathing hard. Something crackled above their heads, and they heard a distant bang.

"Good lord," said Tom. "They're shooting at us. That's illegal." If she'd had the breath, Sara would have laughed at the injury in his voice. The lights fell farther behind, and the shouts were fading. They were safe if they could get off the flats and into some thick woods, a big woods, hopefully, that they could follow across the Cape for miles before they went to cover on the ocean shore.

"Dog," Peter called. He was still behind them. "Decoy."

Tom and Sara separated a dozen feet and stopped. Peter loped between them and halted a few yards past where they stood motionless. Sara heard the dog, breathing hard and snuffling, whether following their scent or just nursing a cold, it was hard to say. Dogs were so full of affectations, learned from their masters, probably, that it was difficult to know when they were serious. The dog saw Peter, though, and its big face lit up with pleasure as it bore down on him. Just before the dog reached Peter, or where he would have been if he hadn't moved at the last instant, Sara moved like lightning. She grabbed at its left forepaw and rolled, as Tom grabbed the right forepaw and did the same. The dog flipped headfirst and thudded solidly on its back. They were off and running before it could catch its breath and were a hundred feet nearer to the woods when it found its voice and squealed like a pig. Peter had crunched the end of its thick tail with a powerful bite that would leave the tail bent and broken.

"Could we perhaps now curtail activities for the rest of the day?" Tom asked with mock formality.

"Certainly," Peter agreed. "How about breakfast?"

"How about chewing on some dried fruit?" Tom suggested.

"Sounds good," Peter said cheerfully. "Thank you, both, again. For what it's worth, we may have saved a human."

"It's okay, Peter. Any time. It's too bad they don't share your reverence for life."

"Some do. Like Thoreau and Schweitzer, a few fruits and nuts." He laughed and took the package Tom handed him. They munched silently. Sara felt almost too tired to eat. She slept, and woke only when her guardian spirit smelled coffee an hour later.

·13·

They passed the morning peacefully, in the same routine as the day before. Sleep and study, food and conversation, and an overnight journey to look forward to. Heavenly, Sara thought, and all for a good cause, too. Last night's escapade was a bit outrageous, of course. Peter would surely get them killed some day, but she couldn't feel bad about it. It was a good feeling saving a life, any life.

"We could make the dunes in a couple of hours," Peter said. "Don't you think we should? We'll be safe enough in these woods."

"I'm sure we should," Tom agreed. "It's just so comfortable here. Okay."

"Sure, let's go." Sara closed her book and slipped it into her pack. "I like the woods in the daylight."

There were trails here, but few hikers. They went slowly and quietly, on the paths and off them, through the friendly bayberry and beach-plum tangles and across the sun-flecked floor of the pitch-pine woods. They had it to themselves except for an occasional chipmunk who scampered out of their way in terror. As if water rats munched barbecued chipmunks on hot dog rolls, thought Sara, laughing to herself. At least the quail ignored them. They skirted a small kettle pond nearly filled with buttonbush and home to a hundred cackling red-winged blackbirds. Their comments seemed uncalled for, considering that rats never did them any harm. Mob psychology of some sort. Featherheads.

"Aren't we going a little out of the way? We could cut straight north from here, toward High Light." Peter was leading, but Sara hadn't lost her sense of direction.

"There's something I want to see. It's not much farther."

"So long as it isn't dangerous," Tom said.

They came to a well-marked path and followed it cautiously down into a hollow. Once they sank into the grass as a human head sailed smoothly by above the brush. A paved bike trail followed the edge of the marsh here.

"Too bad rats don't count as woodland creatures. We could wear flat tails and pose as beavers." They really weren't in any danger, but Tom had a point. They were pushing it a little, to be here in the daylight.

"Not much farther. You'll see." Another fifty feet, and Peter stopped. "There."

Sara couldn't see anything at first. A pool of water.

"The frog?" Tom suggested.

"Not the frog, you ninny. The spring. That's the Pilgrim Spring, where the Pilgrims stopped for water on the way to their rock."

"Oh," Tom said, with greater interest. He inspected the spring. The frog eyed them suspiciously. "It's pretty small."

"It's no geyser, but it smells fresh enough." Peter took a drink. "It's good."

They all drank. Tom looked at the woods around them, not an old woods and certainly not dating back the three-hundred-seventy-and-more years to the first English settlers. "I'd like to believe it."

"The historian's bane," Peter agreed. "The Nausets drank from it, for thousands of years, probably."

"Probably," Tom agreed. "And I suppose they're more our spiritual fellows than the Pilgrims, in a way. They sat lightly on the land, too, and revered it and left it mostly undisturbed. A little too lightly for their own good eventually. The Pilgrims took root and pretty soon took over. If we could learn from both . . ."

"I just think it's nice to make a connection like this," Sara said. "To stand here, or at First Meeting where they met the Indians, and think that only time, a line of sunrises, separates us."

"Me, too," Tom agreed, looking at her as if he had just noticed something. "A lot of sunrises, though." He calculated rapidly. "About a hundred and thirty-five thousand."

"Thanks," Sara said.

"There's more than that that separates us, unfortunately," Peter said. "If we could only learn from each other."

"Deep water, Peter," Tom said.

Peter nodded, and they all silently contemplated the poor

frog, who was nearly catatonic with fear by now and would probably spend the rest of the day staring into the woods at nothing.

"Company," Sara whispered, and they slipped into the brush and continued north as a group of children arrived to admire the spring.

At noon they were high on the ocean bluff with a view of the blue water below. Before them High Light, the white stone lighthouse, clung dangerously close to the edge of the cliff. It would probably be abandoned in a few more years or fall into the sea. It was still in use, though fully automatic now and of little importance to any but the smallest ships. Most ships were equipped with coastal radar. The beacon at High Light was probably still reassuring to returning party boats, however.

There were tourists milling around the buildings. Fences kept them from the dangerous and fragile cliff. The rats had merely to follow a well-worn trail below the fence to reach the stone foundation of the tower. Here they found an elderly rat lounging in a grassy space outside the wall and smoking a corncob pipe.

"Hello."

"Hello, come aboard, friends. I'm Captain Jonathan." The heavy, graying rat rose and put out his large paw. Rats did little traveling except by necessity and were unfailingly hospitable to those who passed their way.

"Thank you. Peter Waterrat, my sister, Sara, and my good friend Tom." Peter briefly explained their mission, and the travelers were invited to stay for lunch.

"In the open air," the captain announced. "Just make yourselves at home here on the veranda."

"Nice place," Sara said.

"None better," the old rat agreed. "Until it falls into the sea, at least. We're sort of living on the edge here, but the view makes it worthwhile. The children have moved on, and it's just my wife and me at the brink of time. Emmy?" he called back into an opening in the foundation. A plump rat blinked out into the sunshine.

"Visitors? How lovely."

Sara asked for a place to wash and glimpsed a mammoth white-walled kitchen hung with pots and pans enough to supply an army. She wasn't surprised to learn that the old rats' children often dropped by at mealtimes. Emmy proved a splendid cook.

They ate at a kind of rough picnic table on the front lawn, as Jonathan had promised. After polite inquiries about their families and their present mission, they were told the history of several generations of the captain's forebears. It was an interesting and in places violent account of great storms and wrecks and rescues, enemy ships and mysterious explosions in wartime, and sightings of outlandish sea creatures. Tom and Sara were fascinated. Peter seemed to be only half listening at times, but he was politely appreciative.

One story in particular commanded everyone's attention. There had been a shipwreck, far enough in the past for the tale to have acquired a few fabulous embellishments, though it had a ring of truth. It was on a cold and stormy January night when the oil in the great lamps that formed the beacon had frozen to sludge and refused to burn. A large ship was driven to shore in the darkness and lay foundering on the shoals. Its passengers and crew feared to take to the furious surf, but they knew the ship was breaking up. On shore the keeper tried in vain to warm the oil on his cooking stove, oblivious to the drama taking place only a few hundred yards to seaward. It was the rats who saved the passengers. A hundred or more migrating rats leaped into the surf and swam safely to shore. They poured up the nearby hollow, seeking food and shelter, and there they were seen by a villager who raised the alarm. A few rats were hunted down and killed, but most escaped and survived to find homes on the Cape. The passengers were rescued by the surfwise fishermen, and for once the rats received some recognition, if little gratitude.

I could tell a better story, Sara thought, the incident of the man on the beach. But of course she couldn't, and she hadn't yet decided whether even to commit it to her diary. It was her story, though, as well as Peter's. Do you write what you would probably never speak of?

They thanked their hosts and promised to stop again on the journey home. The old couple seemed quite emotional in their farewell. If the travelers only could stop back, they'd so like to hear the news from North Cape. They had friends and relatives there, and they loved the dunes, but it had been long since they had seen them, and they were too old to travel now.

Such good people, Sara thought as they waved good-bye, and she and Tom and Peter had given pleasure by their visit. She was glad.

It was less than an hour before they came to the end of the forest. Ahead of them lay the road, with its scattering of houses and motels and the great dunelands curling another ten miles to Cape End. They would have to wait for darkness now.

·14·

They slept. The afternoon was warm and sunny. Insects droned, and hammers thudded in the distance. More building. Where would it end? Peaceful enough here, though. Sara was both surprised and annoyed when a car interrupted her thoughts. The rats had seen the sand road, of course, but it had looked unused. A jeep parked directly below the little sandbank they were camped on. They were quite invisible where they were, no need to move, but the woods wasn't improved by this battered old machine or the two rough-looking men inside it.

She paid no attention to what they said. Young rats hung around the trails and barns in brief fascination with the humans, but if you hear one human conversation, you've heard them all, the saying went—and it was true. The brilliant masters of the universe passed their time in twaddle.

"Listen." Peter never lost interest in anything, of

course. He was unquenchable and quite exhausting at times. "Just listen, please."

The men were puffing on cigars and talking big. Something about the ferry. ". . . leaves at noon. We never came, we never left. We have nothing to do with this place."

"And we'll never come back, either," the other voice said. "It's creepy, all this sand and these weird trees. Why do people want to live out here, anyway? What do they do?"

"The tourists fool around at North Cape, and the natives make money off them. What else? And we take money off the natives. He who eats last eats best, just the way the fishes do it." He laughed.

"I don't like sleeping outside."

"One night. So what? At least it isn't going to rain. We can't take a chance on a motel. We'll eat in town tonight and poke around. They got a movie."

The two talked on awhile about nothing and then fell asleep.

"They're planning to rob a bank tomorrow," Peter reported. "There's a parade in town. The Fourth of July parade. It must have been canceled because of the rain last week. The bank's closed during the parade, and they figure they can just walk out with the money and get lost in the crowd."

"That doesn't sound too smart to me," Tom said. "You go to the end of a sand spit to commit a crime and expect to get away with it?"

"They don't sound too smart, either," Peter said. "How intelligent is crime?"

100

No one had an answer. Crime was out of their experience.

The men started their jeep at dusk and backed up the road toward the highway. Tom immediately began preparations for supper. The meal would be simpler, he said, but he hadn't really meant for them to starve. Peter was unusually quiet, meditating, as Sara knew. This was a bad sign under the circumstances.

Supper was good. A stew of dried cod, onions, and potatoes, with just enough herbs and black pepper to make it interesting. They talked, but Peter was still holding back his thoughts.

"Shouldn't we try to stop them?" He said it finally.

"Why? Reverence for cash?" Tom, too, had sensed what Peter was considering and was ready for him this time.

"Well, no. It's not our business, I guess. But someone could get hurt. They must be armed. And now we know about it. Maybe we could do something."

"We won't even get there until tomorrow night, Peter. It'll be too late to interfere," Tom said calmly. A careful choice of words, Sara thought.

"That's what I've been thinking about. There is a way."

"No trucks, Peter. You know that."

"No, of course not. I didn't mean a truck. I meant a boat."

There was a silence. What boat?

"We could sail from the bay beach to North Cape in a couple of hours in this wind. I saw boats this morning that we could handle."

A sailboat. It was an absurd idea, but what a thought—

just what she'd been wanting. "You really think so, Peter?"

"Sara!" The exasperation in Tom's voice was evident. He was dealing with a pair of idiots.

"You know about sailboats, don't you, Sara?" Peter knew that, of course.

"I've read a lot about sailing. I've never done it. Except fooling around at the pond with Sally. We made a sailboat out of logs and an old shirt. It's not the same exactly."

"It certainly isn't. We could be drowned or washed ashore at Plymouth. We'd get a warmer reception than the Pilgrims." Tom's objections were unconvincing, though. She had the sense that he wouldn't want to disappoint her, an unexpected development. There were other advantages to the plan. Getting around the sand neck to North Cape was no easy trip and the most dangerous part of their whole journey. They'd be able to deliver the insulin a day early, too, and that could make a difference. Lives even. Peter was so logical with his mad ideas.

In the end they agreed at least to look and see what sort of boats might be available. Then they'd decide. They could have a good three hours sailing time before the tide pulled too far out.

They cleaned their campsite, leaving it slightly more orderly than they'd found it, a rat's irresistible temptation to improve on nature. The bay beach was only half a mile through the trees. The houses here were large and few and set artfully into the dunes. They gave an illusion of nature undisturbed, the erratic taste of humans as well, it seemed. There were boats. Most lacked sails and were much too large for them to manage.

Sara saw it first—their boat. It was maybe six feet long,

a kind of sailing dinghy. The sail was furled but still aboard. The boat wallowed heavily at anchor just beyond the gentle surf.

"So," she said brightly.

"That's it, huh?" Tom said. "Are you sure?"

"The wind's right," Sara said. "It would blow us there without a sail. There are even life vests; look. It's all right, Tom."

"You're the captain."

She saw Peter's smile out of the corner of her eye. The captain. A bit of fiction, but it felt good just the same. They swam out and climbed aboard, and she spent the next quarter hour sharing her nautical wisdom with Tom and Peter as they bailed water from the bilge. The boat slowly righted itself and began to bob perkily in the swell. Just in time, before she ran completely out of lore. Sara fiddled with the sail and found it could be raised easily. She stationed her mariners at their posts, ready to swing the boom when she said to, and cut through the anchor rope. The boat swung with the wind, and they were sailing.

It was easy. They ran before the breeze like a water spider with greased toes, Tom said. The little boat seemed to enjoy the experience of sailing itself with no more than ten pounds of skillful crew. They simply flew.

Running with the wind, there was little sense of speed other than the hiss of water on the hull. The swell was light, a gentle rolling and the occasional slap of an ill-timed wave. The dark shore slid past almost imperceptibly, but they gradually drew nearer to the distant lights of North Cape. At the tiller, Sara had no feelings of doubt or fear. She was in control.

"You got your wish." Tom said it.

103

"Yes." No. "It's terrific, isn't it?" What was missing was the sunlight reflecting off converging planes of sky and water and turning spray to gold and silver, the gulls wheeling in the air above, and other boats with brightly colored sails all racing in a celebration of the wind. To live in darkness was the price of survival for rats, the master race, rat race, clever parasites. Were the humans happy in the sun? Not likely. Drinking too much beer to dull their sensibilities and their worries over all the cares they'd meant to leave on shore. Did you ever get your wish, and if you did, then what? But this was terrific in its way. To sail away on a starlit bay. She relaxed. She'd gotten her wish, a little.

They almost made the beach. The keel grounded on the sand a hundred yards from shore. They rocked uncomfortably for a minute and then swam, towing their waterproof and buoyant packs. Their little boat would come to rest on someone's doorstep, no worse for wear.

Kendon lived a quarter mile inland, in the foundation of a three-hundred-year-old barn. The foundation stones had been laid by the Pilgrims or their children, it was said. The stones themselves were old enough.

It was a little past midnight when they approached the weathered building. They had no trouble finding it from Grandfather's directions, as its high peaked roof and lightning rods stood out above the trees on a low hill at the very eastern end of North Cape. Only a few lights marked the broad curve of the harbor, and no cars moved on Main Street at this hour. Farther east and north, the wasteland of Sandy Neck was black as pitch.

"Who's there?" It was a rat's voice, low and almost inaudible to other ears.

"Hello, Kendon?" Peter called from the grass a few yards from the foundation wall. "It's Peter and friends."

"Peter! We didn't expect you until tomorrow. You must have flown."

"Nearly," Peter answered.

They followed a shadowy form through an opening between two blocks of granite and down a short tunnel into a large and comfortable den. Sara looked around her in surprise. The furniture was simple but very beautiful. It was old-style Rattish, long predating the colonists. The walls of the large living room were lined with books. She couldn't see the titles, although there were many in Lucas's distinctive Cape Edition bindings.

"Ah-ha, they've come. And sooner than expected. I hope you took no unnecessary chances, youngsters." Kendon's father rose from his chair by the fire and greeted them.

"We're fine, sir," Peter answered cheerily, "and so's the insulin."

"That's grand, then. We'll take care of it from here, and you can get something to eat and have a bit of sleep if you like. We can talk in the morning."

That was fine with her, Sara decided. She collapsed on the comfortable bedclothes she was offered by Kendon's timid sister Alethia, and after thinking briefly but with satisfaction of their sail, she quickly fell asleep.

·15·

When Sara awoke and made her way to the kitchen, she found a vigorous discussion in progress. Peter's suggestion that they might do something about the impending robbery of the Cape Five Cent Savings Bank had been rejected out of hand by the elders, which was hardly surprising. Only Kendon had kept his silence, in at least token support. Sara knew Peter too well to conclude he had given up altogether, but the talk now was of another matter. The distribution of the insulin had gone smoothly overnight, except in the case of Aunt Ruth. She was often the cause of some disturbance, Sara gathered. This time she had disappeared, leaving only a slip of paper bearing the word *painting*.

"Gone to the dunes, goodness knows where," Kendon's mother said in exasperation. "She was always half mad, you know. I'm afraid there's nothing to be done until she returns."

"How likely is she to come back, if she's that ill?" Peter asked. "Perhaps she doesn't mean to." No one an-

106

swered him, and it was clear that this was in their minds as well.

"You have to understand, Peter, that your great-aunt has tried the patience of her friends and relations at North Cape for all the life of the oldest one of us. She's a very bright and interesting person and a marvelous painter, though her style is certainly unique, but she can be extremely difficult."

"It's good, then, that reinforcements have arrived just in time," Peter said. "I've heard about Aunt Ruth all my life, too, and I'd like to meet her. We could look for her. Tom? Sara?"

Tom nodded from behind his coffee cup. Sara could see he was amused. These good people might know their eccentric artist, but they didn't know Peter as Tom and Sara did. Peter was always diplomatic, though completely truthful, of course, but he never gave up if something mattered to him.

"You can look, Peter, and we'll help. It isn't that we don't care about Aunt Ruth, but there are over ten square miles of dune and scrub forest to search, a nearly impossible task. And you can't even begin until tonight. The town will be thronging with people this morning and quite impassable." Kendon's father was trying hard to be accommodating, Sara felt, but clearly no one else was going to look for Ruth.

"It's the parade," Kendon explained. "You can hear the band practicing. It sounds as if they need it."

Peter let the matter drop, and they talked on amicably, exchanging news of family and life on the Cape. There had been much growth at North Cape in recent years, but little on the fringes of the National Shorelands, where a

107

few old Cape families maintained small farms. A faint whiff of cow occasionally drifted in from the barn above to remind them of their agricultural setting.

After breakfast Kendon offered to take them through the scrub to a field where they could see the parade being organized. They found other creatures hanging about the fringes of the woods as well—birds, rabbits, raccoons even—out late or up early and all trying to appear as if they had just happened to be passing by. Silly creatures. What was wrong with curiosity?

It was a fascinating scene. The humans, whose everyday activities were so often outlandish and extreme, had given themselves a further license to make noise and promote their interests. The amusing thing, Sara thought, was that their celebrations were so ordinary, just the same sorts of things they would do anyway; but maybe that was what they were celebrating, after all.

"There are certainly enough floats with environmental themes," Tom observed. "Not a bad sign."

"A little late, but good to see, I guess," Peter said doubtfully. "They've always been more aware of sitting lightly on the sands out here."

"Since the beginning, I think," Kendon agreed. "They must have clung to existence by their fingernails in those early years. It's a friendly place only if you have things under control."

"Have they yet?" Tom asked, looking with some puzzlement at the mayhem spread out before them.

"Hard to say." Kendon shook his head. "It's a peculiar place, a mix of artists and writers, tourists and hard-nosed commercialism. It's a little gaudy, but it seems to work for them. It's in all their interests to keep the shore lands healthy at least, so we benefit as well.''

Kendon and Peter had much in common, Sara noticed. They were intelligent and decisive in their thinking. A bit sardonic about the humans and yet far more interested in them than most rats, who preferred to ignore the whole outrageous human drama as much as possible and look inward to the thoughts and doings of their own tribes and families.

The parade was forming now, and bands and floats passed slowly beneath their tree as they circled to head off toward Main Street. Sara's sharp eyes saw a peculiar sight many yards away. It was a flatbed truck, an exterminator's float, of all the grotesque things to parade down the street! It held flags and ribbons and cardboard minutemen and, fleeing from their muskets, a pack of papier-mâché rats, full-size and quite convincing at a distance.

What if she hadn't seen it and called their attention to it when she did and given Peter the thirty seconds that were all he needed to assess the situation and make a plan? She'd never know.

''I'm crossing town in that,'' he said flatly, and began to climb down from their safe branch. Tom followed without comment, and Sara waved good-bye to Kendon and followed Tom, unwilling now to be left behind, she realized, however mad the undertaking.

It was easy to jump onto the low flatbed as it brushed the bushes at the edge of the field. Sara found a place between two paper rats and stretched out on a comfortable bed of wood chips. Nothing to it, really. The creatures around them were mounted on old mattress springs and moved quite realistically with the gentle jouncing and swaying of the float. Peter had assumed, rightly it seemed, that the humans wouldn't share a float with mannequins, so they had the truck bed to themselves.

"I should have known you'd follow," Peter said between his teeth, a bit contritely, Sara thought.

"You bet," Tom said, "when you give us ten seconds to make a decision. This is certainly the most idiotic thing you've ever gotten us into. I hope it's not the last."

"Me, too," Peter said.

"It's pretty exciting, though," Sara volunteered. They were speaking softly, moving their mouths as little as possible, though no one seemed to be paying them much attention. The float was moving steadily now, and they felt reasonably inconspicuous among the dozen or so swaying paper bodies. Small groups of people lined the road, and they could hear the rats referred to and even praised for their realism. That was a bit worrying. A band began to play behind them, and further comments were drowned in blatts and oompahs. It wasn't a very good band, but it was loud, another reliable human trait.

For an instant Sara found herself eye to eye with a little girl of four or five, who burst into tears and turned to her mother. Sara forced herself to look away. She could imagine the child saying, "It looked at me, Mommy," and the mother reassuring her that it did no such thing and turning a curious and worried glance on the rats herself. Must be careful of the eyes, and of the children. She hoped Peter would use his good sense and not stare down some hapless human.

It was fascinating. By looking well ahead she could avoid their direct gaze and yet see their faces and expressions. There was great variety in their appearance, she realized. From a distance and in photographs they tended all to look alike. At this close range she could distinguish the different shapes of mouths and noses and see the peculiar ways they cut their hair. Many young people wore shirts with words and pictures on them, some simple and pretty and others totally obscure and even vaguely threatening, she thought. The rats floated past it all unchallenged. Perhaps they were really safe. It would take courage, she realized, to risk being called a fool for investigating a paper rat, however suspicious the thing might look. You could always hide as what you were supposed to be. Peter thought of things like that.

The shop windows were filled with art and clothing, T-shirts, flags, and giant kites such as they liked to watch flying above the beach. Interesting smells of strange and familiar foods wafted from dozens of restaurants and stands. It was exhilarating. She felt positively festive, almost a part of the excitement and gaiety. Almost, indeed!

"The bank," Peter called out over the trumpets. "And the robbers."

It was the robbers all right, wearing dark glasses and dressed in holiday clothing like the others, but unmistakably the two the rats had seen on the sand road. They were standing in front of the bank doors, and each carried a well-filled shoulder bag. As Sara watched, the two moved casually to the corner of the building and one at a time strolled down a small alleyway that ran north from Main Street.

"Now or never," Peter shouted. "Let's go." He leaped from the truck and streaked after the robbers. Sara and Tom followed him as if drawn by magnets. There were shouts and screams as the spectators nearest them tried to get away and crashed into others, who were trying to see what the commotion was about.

The robbers must have believed they'd been discovered and began to run. The rats followed them around the rear of the building and were in time to see the men peel off their shirts and reveal more-brightly colored ones beneath. The bags, too, lost their outer shells and changed shape and color. Caps went on their heads, and the dark glasses came off. The shirts were stuffed hurriedly into the bags, and the men turned at the next alleyway and sauntered back toward Main Street and the parade.

The rats dodged beneath the bank building and lay low as two young men came running and stopped in confusion behind the bank. The rest had apparently lost interest, and the robbery was still undiscovered.

"Damn," Peter said.

"It was a good try, Peter. We did our best. Even those of us who were just hanging on for our lives," Tom added. "That was quite an experience."

"I don't like losing," Peter said.

"I know," Tom agreed with feeling.

"Especially to thieves."

"Human thieves. Not really our affair. We steal their chickens," Tom suggested.

"Not the same."

"We can't solve all their problems, Peter."

"Just this one." He was silent a moment. "They said the noon ferry."

"Yes, but—"

"We can at least look."

"All right."

112

It was simple enough to reach the water by traveling under the buildings and through the many drains and culverts that ran beneath Main Street. The parade had continued despite the brief furor caused by the rats.

The ferry was docked at the end of a long wharf, one of the few left in what was once a thriving harbor. There were a number of ships tied up at the end of the wharf, and a helpful tangle of ropes and lines crossed the oily water. Peter pointed to the heavy braided fenders lining the sides of the passenger ferry. There would be no difficulty getting on board.

"There they are." Sara had seen the robbers first. They were sitting together by the rail, like peas in a pod in their bright green shirts. Were they clever or foolish? Always hard to say with humans. The bench ran along the rail, with space beneath it for life preservers—and for himself, Peter pointed out.

"Why do you feel you have to do this, Peter?"

"Not sure. As I said, I don't like to lose."

Tom wasn't going to give up, either. "That's an interesting reason. Does it outweigh the value your life may have for your family and all the people you could help in the future? We need you to help us find Ruth, too, and we're delaying our search for this."

"I know." Peter looked somewhat chagrined at all this sound reasoning. "It won't take long, and I wouldn't try it if I didn't think it was reasonably safe."

"What about their weapons? What if they shoot someone in desperation or hold passengers hostage?"

"I'll deal with that first."

"Good luck, then, Peter." Sara touched him lightly on the shoulder, and he smiled and slipped into the water.

He was out of sight for a few moments as he swam swiftly underwater to the side of the ship. Sara saw his head appear beside a fender. He looked quickly around him and climbed the heavy rope to the deck and disappeared through a scupper.

Beneath the seat Peter was glad to find that his judgment was correct. He could move easily under the bench, well concealed by feet and baggage. It would be only through bad luck that he would be seen, and there were drain holes offering escape every few feet. He had climbed on at a point directly below the robbers and easily found their colorful bags stuffed partway beneath the seat. He could feel the hard metal of the handguns within each bag. It took only a few seconds to gnaw holes in the light nylon and remove the weapons. They went through the drain and into the water with a faint splash that was unnoticed in the general hubbub of the harbor. The guns left an unpleasant oily taste in his mouth. In another minute he had enlarged the holes in each bag so that bundles of cash were already spilling beneath the seat. He surveyed his work with satisfaction for a moment and then turned and sank his teeth into the nearest ankle of the smaller and, he judged, more excitable of the thieves. The reaction was spectacular, though Peter was down the rope and into the water almost before he heard it. Sara told him when he arrived back below the wharf that the man had rocketed to his feet and out into the middle of the deck, dragging the shoulder bag with him and scattering its contents at the feet of his fellow passengers. His companion had stayed seated but grabbed his own bag, to retrieve his gun perhaps, and managed to strew bundles of money on the deck in front of him.

The other passengers had simply watched this madness

in amazement, too startled to move. The larger robber pointed to the gangway, and they ran for it, but a large and remarkably hairy deckhand had evidently understood and blocked their way.

"Well done, Peter," Tom said, a little ruefully, Sara thought.

"Thanks, Tom. That was all a bit of luck, and I know it. Let's get on with the important things."

They hurried back up the long wharf as the commotion above them grew. It would be hours before the humans sorted out events. Someone might eventually think to investigate the source of the tooth marks on the robber's ankle, but it would remain a mystery. Sara hoped that any rats already on board for the hazardous ride to Bayport would decide to take a later boat.

·16·

They stayed beneath the buildings as far as they could and then traveled north through drains and along gullies as fast as possible. Fortunately, most of the town's inhabitants were still thronging on Main Street in the wake of the parade. They didn't stop until they were deep into a bayberry jungle at the edge of the duneland forest.

"Ruth's den?" Tom asked. The day had begun to cloud over. With the wind from the northeast there could be rain and worse by evening.

"Makes sense," Peter said. "Maybe someone around there would have a suggestion, or we could find another clue. It's a place to start. Better than just roaming the dunes." He looked at the scrub forest stretching north toward the distant ocean beach.

They found Aunt Ruth's den where Kendon's precise directions had put it, on a wooded hillside overlooking the harbor. Inside, the walls were covered, quite literally,

116

with countless canvases, many mirroring the view above in every light and mood. The paintings lay in piles on the floor as well. Sara gasped at their beauty and strangeness. Some were naturalistic, almost photographic in their realism, though more whole and alive than any photograph. Others were strange blossoms of color and design, the children of the harbor and the dunes and forest still, perhaps, but unearthly and unreal. They were quite lovely, Sara thought, though she could see why some Cape Enders might question Ruth's sanity. And where was the artist?

The small kitchen was clean and neat. On the table an unwashed coffee cup held down the one-word note, *painting*. Painting certainly, but where?

They cruised in and out of rooms, finding paintings, paints, and canvases in nearly every one, and then back to the main parlor, the studio really, the largest room with the most paintings and an ingenious opening through which the watery remains of daylight now shone on an empty easel. They stopped here, baffled for a moment, until suddenly Peter went and stood before three almost identical impressionistic paintings of a dune and a curve of beach beyond.

"These are still wet. If she's been working on a series, perhaps she's gone back to the same place."

"Worth a try," Tom agreed. "Hadn't we better look for some food? I'm not going to be able to explore the dunes on an empty stomach. Where is that place?"

"The north shore," Sara said. "I remember the curve and the two low hills from the map. She's looking down from a higher hill, a dune that's a bit farther in from the beach. We can take a compass reading and head straight for it.''

"Good.'' Peter looked appreciatively at his sister. "Good thinking.''

"Thank you,'' she said, and felt a glow. She didn't look at Tom.

"We can start at dusk,'' Peter continued, "which will be earlier in this weather. We can take it slow and careful and be there by midnight.'' He was silent a moment. "They could have figured this out. Why didn't they?''

"I had the sense they were a little tired of her, Peter,'' Tom suggested cautiously. "Of her eccentricity and her utter independence, maybe. Who knows? She must be very old.''

"Mmm, older than Grandfather and a character apparently even when she was young. But very much alive a few days ago at least. Look at those paintings. Nothing old about them.''

They napped for an hour. Hunger woke Tom first, and he explored Ruth's pantry. He turned on the radio and happily assembled a good stew of salted meat and vegetables while he listened to a Mozart symphony. The pleasant sea breeze that had cooled the Main Street parade had gradually increased to a steady wind, and a thick mist now surged through the stunted forest above them. Peter and Sara awoke to find their supper waiting.

"The radio says a northeaster, Peter.'' Tom was matter-of-fact. They would go on, of course, but it would be no jaunt.

"Nasty,'' Peter agreed. "We'll carry all the supplies

and equipment we can and set up a shelter if we have to. She must have a place out there.''

''I guess, but what sort of shelter is there in the dunes? No holes, no rocks, just stunted little trees.''

Tom was right, Sara thought. And for once his attitude seemed nearer to gloom than his usual realism. Peter was confident but quiet. They'd not ordinarily go on the land in this sort of weather. There was rarely any need to, for rats everywhere kept their storehouses full as much as possible and had well-made plans for every likely emergency. Storms were fun to watch from a warm and safe vantage point. Sara had seen the wind-driven waves roll over bar and beach and come to roil the marsh itself, and once she'd stayed with cousins in the timbers of the old Coast Guard station and watched yards of sea cliff tumble into boiling surf. The wind hissed above them now, but later it would howl as it came lashing through the dunes and driving sea spray, twigs, and sand before it.

''Best get started.'' Peter slung his pack over his shoulder and looked at the others. They picked up their own packs and followed him out into the dusk.

It wasn't bad yet. The wind in their faces was strong and wet with mist, but there was still no rain. The air smelled strongly of the sea, of the bottom of the sea, Sara thought grimly. Something awful this way comes.

Peter's compass led them on a difficult path, through heavy brush and up and down steep sandy hills. They skirted several small bogs, the buttonwood and bulrushes seeming out of place in this sandy land, like palm-shaded oases in the Sahara. Sara was glad to travel in the lee of Tom's greater bulk as the wind began to moan above them.

119

It grew darker still, and the storm began to drown all other sound. Sara thudded into Tom's substantial flank. Peter had stopped to fix a rope between them.

"We should go on while we can, I think," he shouted, "but there's no need to take a chance on getting separated." They each clipped the dark green nylon line to their packs, and they continued on. Sara felt a little safer now, drawing strength and comfort from the line as if it were a kind of power cord.

The rain began, a torrent, blinding and nearly suffocating them as it splattered on their muzzles and drenched their bodies, driving through their thick fur and chilling the skin beneath. Still, it was a summer storm, cold but not life-threatening. The pines bent and writhed in the howling blasts that now came ashore from the angry ocean, but they artfully slipped and dodged the worst where other trees would break or be uprooted.

Lightning struck on the hill beside them, lighting up the wind-whipped forest for an instant; Sara was nearly knocked to the ground by the ear-splitting crack of thunder. There was nothing now to do but struggle on. No place here to shelter. She felt a moment's fear. Rats were tough, but she'd never been in a storm like this. Peter and Tom would take care of her. No, she could take care of herself and do her part.

They were slowing down, and that was just as well. She was starting to wobble on her legs and was near the end of all her strength. They'd soon have to stop to rest, but they should also be nearing the northern shore. She could hear nothing but the roar of the storm, though she thought she could sense the pounding of the surf at times. Could she really feel it through the ground? The land beneath their feet was so liquid that it was hard to tell the sand from sodden wind. They were in another depression now and soon they were slogging through water to their knees.

She heard Tom's shout, above even the howling wind, and almost instantly she felt the ground give way beneath her paws, and she was wallowing on her chest in sandy mud. Quicksand? That was something in old jungle pictures. She could barely move and made no progress as she tried to churn forward through the soup of sand and waterweed. Would they sink further? Could they drown, or would they just die of exposure here in the cold water and the wind?

They drew together even though they couldn't hear their own words in the constant roar. It was like a thousand trumpets blowing a single note. In a flash of lightning she saw Tom's face, blank with helplessness, and her brother's, pained with guilt. If she could only speak to him and tell him it wasn't his fault, not this time. They had all wanted to find Ruth, all felt they had to try, despite the coming storm. It was her fault, really. If she hadn't recognized the place from the map, they'd have roamed the dunes, keeping to the higher ground, and not have foundered in the bog. It was Tom's fault, even, for dragging them down with his bulk, his strength useless without solid ground to stand on. They were sinking, she was sure of it, or the bog was filling in the torrent. She could feel the cold water creeping up her flanks. How much time did they have? Was there nothing they could do? If they could only speak to one another. She tried to shout, but she hardly heard herself.

Something hit her on the back. A branch? She didn't turn to look until she felt a second stinging blow. She turned her head with difficulty and saw only darkness, and then in a flash of lightning she saw the rope, a heavy braided rope that was whipping in the wind. With a tremendous effort she turned her body in the slush, feeling her back legs sink deeper still, and groped in the dark for the flailing line. It hit her across the snout, and she cried in pain, but then she had it. Had anything in all her life felt so good and so solid? She pulled, and it held. It was fast somewhere above on the rim of the sand kettle. Was there someone there? There must be. A rope out of nowhere was just too unlikely otherwise.

Quickly Sara began to haul herself along with all her remaining strength. It was like trudging through molasses, through cold oatmeal, but handhold by handhold she was moving. She felt the line holding her back. Tom would feel it, too. She pulled until her arms ached, and then the rope eased behind. Tom had realized she was moving. She felt his paw on her side. He had seen the rope in the lightning flashes and caught it as well. He pulled even with her and thumped her on the shoulder as he went past. She could feel Peter pulling on the rope behind her. She felt safe now, exhausted but safe, attached to something solid up ahead in the darkness.

The climb seemed to take forever. It couldn't be that far. It wasn't, surely, but progress was hand over hand and foot by foot. She was out of the water finally and climbing the steep side of the little hill. The slope leveled gradually, but Tom kept moving forward. She could see nothing in the lightning flashes except stunted trees, and then a huge distorted figure beckoning them. Stories of wraiths and mole men flashed through her mind, and she was afraid, but Tom kept moving, and then they were at the mouth of a tunnel. No tunnels in the sand, Tom had said, but in they went, and the roar of the storm was behind them, and it was gone as they stepped into a warm and cheerful fire-lit room beneath the dunes.

"Dr. Waterrat, I presume?" A very old rat stood drying herself before the fire.

"Peter Waterrat, William's grandson; my sister, Sara, and my friend Tom. You seem . . . not unwell, Aunt Ruth?"

"A mission of mercy. I rather thought so. No, my boy, I'm not dead yet, fortunately for you. I do appreciate your coming, all of you. A brave if harebrained enterprise. Perhaps you didn't know about these storms?"

"Not exactly, I guess," Peter said. "I'd read about them, but. . . ."

"Not the same as being in one, no. They've finished off many a shipwrecked sailor who thought he'd come to land and safety."

Peter had rummaged in his pack and found the insulin.

"Thank you, Peter. I had medicine for only another day, so you're just on the mark. Here, have some towels and dry yourselves. I have coffee and tea. A little brandy? The worst thing for you, but it's what I like when I'm chilled to the bone. What a lovely coat, my dear."

"Thank you, Aunt Ruth," Sara found herself saying meekly. This was absurd—the rescuers rescued, and by an annoyingly hearty little old creature. No wonder her family thought her insufferable, and yet Sara found that she liked Aunt Ruth immensely.

"Thank you," Peter said, "for our lives. How did you know we were there?"

123

"Saw you," Ruth said. "I like to look out at the storm. It's like a series of photographs in the lightning flashes. I remember them, you see. My memory is quite stuffed with images, but I'm reluctant to give them up. And suddenly there you were, a pile of half-drowned rats in my own bog. I imagined you'd prefer the parlor on a night like this."

"How—" Tom began, looking at the paneled walls about them.

"A ship, young man. A jolly little sloop buried in the dunes a century ago. I have the log. I chanced on it when I was young and roaming these hills for the joy of it. I've made it my hideaway and studio ever since. It travels still. It sails the billows of the sand, but slowly."

Sara sat with her friends before the fire while Peter briefly told their tale. A mug of hot tea with just a little brandy in it warmed her throat, and gradually the chill went from her limbs and paws, and her teeth stopped chattering. The storm still roared in her head, but it, too, was calming. They had survived.

"I know what you're thinking, Peter. I know faces; it's my trade. You all feel a bit the fools for being rescued by the oldest rat in North Cape. I've lived quite beyond my time, outlived my friends and contemporaries by too long." She looked wistful for a moment. And then she looked at them, at each of them in turn, Sara felt.

"What you don't see, children, not yet, is that life is not a well-staged drama." She smiled. "Your radio message and the journey with the insulin is not a story that had to end in just a certain way. My seeing you wasn't ordained by any master craftsman, though there is one, I am sure of that. Such beauty can be no accident. You followed your compass needle, and I enjoyed my storm, and we chanced on each other. Life is what it is, a story certainly, and a very good one, but always on the first page for us. We are warming by the fire, and outside a great storm is bending the pines, but they know how to bend, and tomorrow's dawn will be calm and clear. I promise you.''

She thought a moment. ''You wanted experience, Peter, and you found it.'' Ruth sipped her brandy and contemplated the fire. ''You also nearly outreached your luck,'' she continued, not looking at them now. ''We are fragile creatures, really, even I. I've pushed my luck, and here I am, old and at the edge of the world. And by heaven, here you come, young and handsome and full of life. I don't deserve you in the least, but I'm thoroughly delighted to have you all. Just think.'' She paused again. ''What if you had gone down in the bog, three new and shiny lives lost to save one old and nearly done? I'd have been quite annoyed with you.'' She laughed. ''So you saw my den, did you? What did you think?''

Sara waited a moment, and when no one else spoke she said, ''I . . . I thought the paintings were wonderful. More alive than life.''

''Oh-ho, you know how to warm an old heart on a cold night. You've an eye for beauty. That's how I see them, too. And I take little credit for them. I was merely the copyist of images that formed themselves. I'm glad you enjoy my paintings. You must choose and take what you like when you go. Take one for William, too. We used to explore these hills together when we were children. You can simply roll them up like wrapping paper and put them in your bag.''

They talked on awhile. Ruth asked about their lives and the news from the mid-Cape and seemed genuinely interested. She told them a little more about her lifetime of painting at Cape End, a small world literally, of people and sand, ships and stunted trees, but infinite in its detail, a great encyclopedia of existence, she said. No need to travel further. Despite her fascination, Sara felt herself sliding into sleep and gladly accepted Ruth's offer of a quiet cabin and warm bedclothes and oblivion.

Sara woke, one more time, she thought dramatically, here at the end of the Cape, the end of the world, to the smell of coffee brewing. There was no one in the kitchen, but a large pot stood warming on the stove, and she poured herself a mug. She found the others out on a rough wooden deck enjoying the promised day.

The sun was up and had turned the dunes to parchment. The little trees seemed painted by some ancient eastern master, and the heavy sea rolled on in even waves and crashed regularly upon the beach with a dull and distant roar. No one spoke to her, and she followed their gaze to the horizon, searching for what they saw, and then she saw it, too, the head and back and giant flukes of a great gray whale as it rose and fell and disappeared beneath the sea, and the image ever after filled a corner of her mind.

·17·

"Morning." Peter must have heard her.

"Morning." The spell was broken.

"Cleared off beautifully," Ruth said. In the morning sunlight she looked and sounded like a pleasant little creature. The commanding figure of the night before was gone, temporarily at least. "I thought you might sleep longer, dear. I wake early now, whether I want to or not, but I like the morning light. We have it all to ourselves out here. They're not allowed on the dunes, a remarkable bit of abstention for them. Get yourselves some breakfast when you like. I won't wait on you, but there's plenty."

"I'll take care of it," Tom said, and disappeared down the tunnel. His usual generosity and a raging hunger, Sara surmised.

"I slept wonderfully," Sara said. "No dreams. I never woke once. I feel reborn."

"As well you might. Looks mild enough this morning, doesn't it?" Ruth pointed down into the little hollow where the bog lay green and cheerful in the morning light. Blackbirds congregated on the bushes. Sara looked and could make no connection with the horrors of the night before, it was so calm and ordinary now.

"Must you return right away, or can you spend a day with me enjoying your new life?" Ruth was speaking to all of them, but Sara sensed it was mainly her Ruth meant. "I'm quite used to solitude, but I find I like your company. It's been a while since I had friends and family to talk with. There's more of interest out here than you might think." She was simply asking, Sara realized, making no assumptions and no imperious demands as they might have expected.

"Certainly, we'll stay a day, Aunt Ruth. I'm sure we'd all like to, and we need the rest after yesterday," Peter answered for them. "I'd like to see Kendon again, too, before we leave North Cape. Our visit with him was cut short rather suddenly, I'm afraid."

"Could we send a letter home so that they don't worry?" Sara asked.

"Write a note after you've had your breakfast, and Tim can take it to town for you and slip it in the post." She must have caught a startled look. "Tim is a student of mine. Coming along quite well, though he lacks boldness. He'll be out this morning with provisions, and to see whether I'm still among the mortals. I'm not quite the old fool they say I am," she added mischievously.

Sara glanced at Peter. Would he let this pass? She doubted it.

" 'A bit mad' was the way I heard it. I think they feel both exasperation and wonder, and perhaps a little envy."

"Most likely, Peter." She smiled at him. "You don't frighten easily, do you?" Peter just shook his head.

Tom reappeared with a tray of eggs and bacon, buttered toast, and a full pot of coffee. "We've pretty well cleaned you out of breakfast stuff."

"No matter. Tim can make another trip if necessary. Students have to earn their toast and butter somehow."

It was a splendid day. The force of the hot July sun was buffered by a cool sea breeze, and the distant puffy clouds served only to emphasize the immensity of sky and sea. Gulls and terns soared above them in the dune drafts, more in idle pleasure than in search of food. They saw no more whales, but many boats and ships came around Cape End or crossed the far horizon.

"We'll take a picnic to the beach when Timmy comes," Ruth said with satisfaction.

"The beach?" Even Peter was startled by this.

"The beach. It's ours, as I've said. You could set a watch for hawks, though I've rarely seen one. No need to take chances at your age. And what else would bother us? You'll see. You never spend a day at the beach down your way, I suppose?" It was only half a question. Sara shook her head.

The promised Timmy arrived as they still drank coffee and lolled in the sun on Ruth's doorstep. He was a roundish little fellow, Peter's age or perhaps a year or two older. He was laboring now beneath an enormous pack as he hauled himself up the last steep slope. Not her image of a rodent Botticelli, Sara considered, but what was what it seemed to be out here?

"Gracious, Tim. What a load." Ruth greeted him with pleasure.

"Thought"—Tim puffed—"you all"—and drew a breath—"might need some extra. I've brought the medicine as well, in case. . . ." He left the thought unfinished.

"All here, all safe, but thank you, Tim. Thank you for everything. Was there much of a fuss?"

"Not really, no. They were a little miffed I knew where to find you. 'If they had known,' etc. And I don't know who they blamed more, me or you," he added with an innocent smile. "I brought fresh corn and bluefish."

"Splendid. We'll have a clambake. Bring your pack down to the kitchen. And, Tom, come along and help me with the pots."

Peter looked at his sister and beamed as the others filed into the den after Ruth.

"You're loving this, aren't you, Peter?"

"Aren't you? She's a kind of national treasure, though I can see why her neighbors shy away. Fancy a clambake in broad daylight. I hope she really knows what she's doing and isn't just gaga in an obscure way."

Sara shook her head firmly. "She isn't crazy. It must be all right."

They all carried something, fish and vegetables, pots and plates. They needed only a beach umbrella to complete the picture, Sara thought. A narrow path led down the hill and through an elfin forest and then a maze of hummocks from which grew beach grass and brambles.

The beach itself was fairly narrow here. They could plop down in the sand a few feet from the safety of the grass

130

and still feel the coolness of the waves. Tim dug the fire pit while all but Ruth gathered the driftwood that had dried already in the sun and wind. Tom loaded the pot with corn dipped in seawater, onions and potatoes, cloves of garlic, and sprigs of fresh dill and parsley. Sara and Peter dug clams at the water's edge, where they were plentiful on this unfrequented shore. The bottom of the fire pit was filled with stones, big ones worn smooth by the washing of the surf, and on them Tim built an almost smokeless driftwood fire.

Later Sara stood at the farthest reach of the waves, where hissing water pulled at her legs and paws. The warmth on her back and the cool water beneath, the enveloping sound of surf and wind was hypnotic, an emptying and a renewal. She could almost feel herself drawing strength from the wild energy of the sea, here, as Peter once said, at the edge of wilderness. All an illusion, probably. Nature begins everywhere, and there's nothing pure about it. The ocean might well be filled with the pale confusion of thought—heady whales, pondering jellyfish, and raging sharks. She swam a little, close in to the beach, and was tumbled roughly by the surf. She was a fine swimmer, far more at home in the water than any human, but unable to float on the crest of thundering breakers like a seabird. She let herself be washed on shore, a sodden lump of flotsam. The others were swimming, puttering, and talking. She stretched out full-length just above the falling tide and began to dig idly in the sand. The hole quickly became a courtyard, with a wall and moat, and a castle grew in the middle almost by itself. Sticks became bridges, cannon, and flagpoles flying seaweed streamers. Tom came to watch and then to begin his own fortifications, and finally Peter joined them, and the future fabric of the Middle Cape fired seeds and pebbles at one another's sand forts as Aunt Ruth looked on benignly. Then Peter took over the watch from Tim, and Tim drew sketches of the rats at work.

"It's done." Tom had unburied the big pot and sampled the ingredients. The clams came first, and empty shells quickly piled up on the sand.

"Nothing quite so good," said Tim, and it was true. Each flavor was distinct and yet shared qualities of all the others. They ate like hungry rats until everything was gone, then dozed or read through the early afternoon.

Sara took her turn at watch, the only one of them, she knew, who could really see a hawk circling eight hundred feet above them. It would see them only as splotches on the sand. There were no such patterns printed in its tiny brain, no rodent cookouts at midday.

Peter seemed to be asleep, but Ruth gazed peacefully at the far horizon, seeing something beyond even Sara's sharp eyes, perhaps.

"Tim's sketches are awfully good, Aunt Ruth."

"Yes. He'll be a fine artist. He is already. He has the talent." She paused. "But more than that he has the will and dedication. He's small and chubby and a little slow in some ways. Just a normal, cheerful, and rather pedestrian lad in everything but art. Many of them were, you know, the great ones. As an artist—" She stopped and suddenly became more stern, a hint returning of the apparition of the storm. "As an artist he is completely dedicated to his work. It draws and drives him, and he gives to it everything he is and has. It's a good thing to remember"—her voice softened again—"child."

Peter's eyes were open, Sara saw. He'd been listening, but he didn't speak.

They were hungry again by supper time and enjoyed canned pork and beans, from a case that had washed up on the beach, Ruth said. These were nowhere near as good as Grandmother's, Sara thought. Later they sat in Ruth's ship before a driftwood fire and talked as Sara felt she'd rarely talked before. Ruth never again spoke with the same quiet passion Sara had heard momentarily on the beach, but the shadow of her work was in all she said. She asked them about their lives and goals, and Sara, somewhat to her surprise, found herself saying that she liked to write. Fortunately, no one pressed her to say more. They talked of Peter's studies. Ruth proved to know a great deal about science for someone of her age and interests.

She talked little about herself, unusual in the elderly, Sara thought. They so often think and talk about the past more eagerly than about the world around them. But when Sara mentioned her grandfather's reaction to *Moby Dick*, Ruth laughed heartily and told a story. She and William had done more than roam the dunes, she said. They had also infiltrated the town and explored the wharves, which were far busier in those days. They grew quite bold in scavenging fish, though only the scraps and throwaways, nothing that would upset the fishermen and draw attention to their forays. But they were young and inexperienced, and they learned one lesson in a frightening and remarkable way.

They had gone out long before dawn, to scrounge what they could from a large and colorful Portuguese trawler. They were admiring their catch of squid and sea bass when the boat was boarded by its full crew, and they found themselves at sea before there was any possibility of escape. They hid in the far corner of the bilge and resigned themselves to a long and uncomfortable day of waiting. They had still more to learn of seamanship, however, and within an hour in the rough and rolling sea, a boat hook had pried two deathly seasick water rats from their hiding place, and they swayed drunkenly in the center of a ring of laughing fishermen. They expected to be flung overboard, alive or dead, and were almost too sick to care. But the men just left them where they crouched and went back to their tasks. The sickness passed, but they were afraid to move and simply watched the men at work.

When it was time for lunch, the fishermen shared their bread with the rats and addressed them familiarly, almost as shipmates. They were mystified until it emerged from the men's talk that rats were considered lucky on board a ship, though it was rare that any would be found on a small fishing boat, and seasick rats at that. Just what might happen when they returned to dock was quite unclear. Rats on shore might well be thought less beneficial. They didn't wait to see, but jumped ship before they touched the wharf, and swam to safety.

Ruth avoided the town after that, but she never forgot her day with the fishermen. They were good and simple men, she felt, who loved and respected the natural world around them as she did. Even back then, however, it was clear that it was not these men who had inherited the earth.

Ruth had watched and studied humans ever since, and though her judgments were hard, they were clear and penetrating. Rats, she felt, could learn far more from humans than mere technology. They could learn values, too, and wonder, boldness, and curiosity. Tom listened carefully.

In the morning Ruth woke them. She had fixed them breakfast, she said, so that they could get an early start and cross the paths before the hikers came. Almost shyly she asked if they each would like now to pick one of her canvases, small ones that could be rolled and tied to their packs, and they accepted her offer with pleasure and confusion. Sara selected a view of the dunes and beach from Ruth's ship and another for her grandfather. Tom picked a painting of the harbor at North Cape, and Peter took a wildly impressionistic little work, a strange amalgam of sand and weathered fence. It reminded him of Bach, he said.

"You can't go without my blessing," Ruth said as they stood at the entrance to the burrow with their packs already strapped on. "You've given me more pleasure than you know, and a bit of hope for the world." She considered them a moment and then spoke again. "Don't expect too much from life. What comes to you will come. But it's always in your power to give. Give your best, and you'll have no regrets. Well then, my dears, cheerio. You'd better be on your way. And do come back."

They promised to return and meant to, though none of them knew when or how. Ruth sent them off with hugs and kisses, and they walked into the dawn, each thinking his or her own tumbled thoughts.

·18·

The sun was up. The day was fine again, warmer than the day before, but clear and bright. The travelers woke from their private musings to talk and laugh. It was a delight to travel through the sandy woods, so different in the pleasant light from their last desperate journey in these hills. Later they saw bikers flying down the paths as if chased by demons, as perhaps they were, and two girls on horseback. One horse turned a worried eye toward the brush that hid them from the riders. They felt quite safe, though abroad in daylight, which was a novelty in their cautious lives. Safe and moving in the dappled sun across soft sand and through the sparkling greens of grass and bough. Quite marvelous.

It was dark when they saw the barn, and they were just in time to join Kendon and his family for the evening meal.

Kendon's father raised his head and broke the moment of silence. "So, a successful journey in every way. Pour the wine, Alethia. We're all most thankful. You liked our

Ruth, I gather? Your Ruth as much as ours, though I'm a cousin, too. She's enriched our lives." He left it at that. "Can you stay with us awhile?"

"Thank you. A day at most, I think," Peter said. "We've been away nearly a week. We have our studies." A bit neglected in the past two days, he could have added.

"I have something to show you tomorrow," Kendon said. "It may surprise you." That was intriguing. Kendon was nice, Sara thought, but a little frightening in his intensity. He was a year older than Peter and deep in the study of physical chemistry, a field of nearly pure research among the rats, though there must be uses for it, she supposed. Original investigations were a bit limited by the lack of elaborate apparatus, although her father did a great deal on a small scale in his lab. She'd heard him say that their lack of need for practical applications gave them an advantage over humans, who could rarely pursue their curiosity unhindered.

Kendon also had a sense of irony that was rather sharp, though never quite unkind. She decided she preferred Tom's quieter good humor.

The amazing aroma that had greeted them still yards from the entrance to the den had proved to be a caldron, nothing less, of mushroom soup. It was even better than Grandmother's, which she'd thought was as good as soup could be.

"Our business," Kendon joked. "We have the manure, Dad figured, so why not make use of it. We grow a nice strain of *Agaricus* for the whole of Cape End. You could take some spores when you go," he offered, and Tom nodded enthusiastically.

They talked on about family and Cape affairs. What a

137

peculiar economy they had, Sara mused. There was no structure to it, really. Makeshift and generosity was all. Giving, as Ruth said. It was their equivalent of taxation, she supposed, but more like manna from heaven in its effect, or the miracle of the loaves and fishes. The humans were smart enough. Why were they so blind in this respect?

The miracle in this case was fresh salmon with sprigs of dill, the gift of friends from near the wharf who'd heard of the visitors. Several other families stopped by during the evening to bring food and thank the travelers for their mission. It was a bit exhausting finally. Sara went to bed.

They slept late the next morning and ate a mammoth breakfast. Sara felt caught up at last, after days of traveling on too little sleep. Kendon proudly showed them around his family's handsome den and then took them above to see the barn.

"These are the original timbers, we think. The darker ones were replacements." Kendon was playing schoolmaster and enjoying himself thoroughly. "We have an early drawing that shows the cupola, without the lightning rods, of course. Those were a late-eighteenth-century addition. You'd wonder such solid and sensible people could be convinced a barn which had already stood a hundred and fifty years was in any danger."

"They'd have felt such fools, I suppose," said Tom, "if they hadn't been, and their barn had burned."

"Over time they may have been right," Kendon agreed. "We're the highest point between the lighthouse and the monument to the Pilgrims at Plymouth."

"Plymouth must have looked pretty good to them."

"Maybe, Tom. A safe harbor, water, good hardwood.

Also unfriendly Indians, cold, and fever. It wasn't paradise quite yet.''

"They came back, though, some of them, from Plymouth. Why was that?''

"More contention probably. They must have been a contentious crew. Struggling with God can't have left them with much patience for their fellow humans. They came here to have the freedom to practice religious oppression and were always surprised when there were further rebellions.''

"Idiots,'' Tom said.

"Not quite,'' Kendon said, "just human. They brought a lot of ideas in their baggage as well, and some of those became the building blocks of this country. Solid ones like these foundation stones. A personal relationship with God also implied individual responsibility within their small world.''

"You like them,'' Sara said.

"Can't help it,'' Kendon agreed. "For all their narrowness, they were brave and bold. They were pioneers as much and more than the Davy Crocketts, a civilized people crossing a stormy ocean to settle in a new and pretty savage land. It's a wonder they kept all they did of their values and beliefs, not to mention their Greek and Latin.''

Sara touched a post and thought about what it represented, wood and craftsmanship and another link with the past, a human-made link. Trees were lovely but imperfect shelters if you were much larger than a water rat. Posts had to be cut square from larger trees, of course, but these were cut well and true for other reasons, too, perhaps. Maybe to express a personal taste and spirit or to please the God of heaven and of the tree. The South Seas islanders were careful, she recalled, to place their hut posts right side up to avoid offending the wood. Why not? Why live in an angry house if you could avoid it?

"I promised to surprise you, and as nice as these old beams may be, they're no revelation. Come."

They followed Kendon back to the den and into the big library chamber, half again as large as theirs at the marsh. What voracious appetites for knowledge these rats had. He opened a glass case and removed a small, dull-looking volume and handed it to Tom.

"We found it here in the barn, tucked away in a crack in the foundation. No author's name, but obviously a child of the first settlers. She's known no other life, and she loves the land. You don't really get that from the writing of the elders. They had other concerns, less worldly and more so, God's will and the harvest. This one was too young for any of that, I think. Our theory is that she was sick or crippled. Probably she died young, and the diary was left hidden. Anyway, she somehow had the time to learn to see the forest and the dunes and even the creatures they shared them with, even rats. She says mice, but she must mean rats. I think she floated very briefly on the surface of their society and left it before they could make her one of them." He looked thoughtful for a moment. "Take it with you if you will, Sara, and show it to Lucas. Just don't lose it, and bring it back someday."

"It will be another reason to come back," Sara said. She took the volume from Tom and put it carefully in her shoulder bag. Tom had a peculiarly pensive look, she thought.

They spent a peaceful afternoon visiting with relatives. Peter and Kendon disappeared into Kendon's small lab for an hour before supper, and Peter emerged looking unusually serious. It came out in their table talk that night that Peter was more impressed than ever with Kendon's scientific knowledge and perhaps shaken by his own relatively slower progress. Another side of Kendon showed itself as well. He as much as admitted to frequent frustration. The physical world, he found, was reluctant to give up its secrets.

"Is there such a desperate need to understand?" Tom asked finally. "I mean, isn't the task infinite in a way?"

"I think there may be a need," Kendon answered, "depending on how you feel about our world. The danger looming ahead isn't any ice age to be weathered over centuries. It may come more like the turning of a page. But that's almost beside the point for me. Anyone who wants to understand his life is in a losing race with time. Isn't that so, Tom?" Tom made a vague gesture of acknowledgment.

·19·

They started back that evening. Dark was always the safest time to travel, and there was no hurry now. They'd follow their usual routine of travel, sleep, and study and be back at home by the end of the week. It had been a highly successful trip, Sara thought, and yet she felt dissatisfied. She had written nothing in her journal since the first day. They had been busy, of course, but that wasn't the whole reason. She was still reluctant to commit herself. What had she expected from the trip?

The weather was good, and the journey along the ocean beach was an easy one. At night the alien force of the Atlantic was felt more strongly than in the day. No one built sand castles in the dark. Sara shivered inwardly and edged a bit higher on the sand. They walked in silence.

They reached the forest shortly after midnight and found the comfortable sand bank where they'd overheard the robbers only four days earlier. It seemed a much longer time. The adventure was over, she supposed. The trip would be tame enough from here. It was just as well. She'd begun to feel a longing for comfortable routines and home. Sleep came easily.

It was one of the best of Cape mornings when she awoke. The others were still asleep, and the land was hers alone. There were no sounds but bird songs and the wind. The crows were the loudest, as usual, but their raucous barks and caws seemed cheerfully at home in the sparkling forest. A dove had something long and dull to say, and in the background a thousand peeps and chugs and chirps and twitters came from the largely invisible chorus of chickadees, finches, and catbirds. A starling flew by, chuntering with pointless rage, and a gull glided high and silent above the trees. Now a light breeze moved the leaves of the stunted oaks and wove a soft sound through the pines. The sun was up already, lighting the long straw-and-gold grass tips and glinting off the wet green blades below. A catbird landed soundlessly a few feet away and looked at her with expressionless eyes from beneath its tonsure. It pecked at the ground and carried something in its mouth as it flew away, a twig perhaps, so as not to appear foolish and unwary to a rat. A rabbit appeared briefly at a distance, and chipmunks twitched across the sandy ground in front of her as if she were only a harmless soft brown rock.

Across the clearing, a stand of larger trees rose forty to fifty feet, each an individual with its trunk twisting artfully and its limbs achieving their own strange and haphazard balance. Each had its story to tell, of storms and nestings, seasons ending and renewed. Above her, the high cirrus clouds majestically carried fragile patterns across the pale-blue sky. It was the same woods she'd awakened to all her life, and yet every bush and tree and blade of grass and every bird and animal in this place was strange to her. It was only the patterns that she knew, but she knew these so well that she would know which shade and color followed which and what each bird would say and do. She would have known this just as well a thousand years before, she supposed, ten thousand, maybe. Would she see the patterns still a hundred years from now? Would anyone? Could she write of what she saw so clearly, capture it for others, defend and represent it and give it a voice? She simply didn't know.

They spent a quiet morning studying and had little to say to one another.

After lunch, Sara began to read the diary of the Pilgrim child and found it as fascinating as Kendon had promised. It wasn't long, but each elegantly penned word seemed to bear a double weight, revealing both the teller and the tale. She had been a lonely child, most at home on the dunes and walking on the ocean beach, though gradually her trips grew shorter as she weakened. Unlike the only other Puritan chronicle Sara remembered having read, the diary rarely mentioned God at all. And yet there was a sense of presence in every line and of companionship on every walk. This was a child in touch with deity, though her people probably never knew it. She also saw and understood the world around her. "The mouse," she wrote, "lives with her family beneath the barn, so that it is her barn as well as ours. She is a beautiful creature who knows well how to thrive in this marvelous and cruel country where we do not. Perhaps she has learned to love it more than we, and that has made the difference.''

Finally Sara closed the little book and handed it to Tom, who as nearly pounced on it as was possible with courtesy. She looked deep into the pine woods, silent and golden in the afternoon sun, and smiled. Now she knew what she was meant to do.

They read and napped, and Sara wrote for an hour in her journal. They started out again late in the afternoon and arrived at the lighthouse shortly before dusk. Captain Jonathan greeted them like family and bustled them into the cozy den. "Emmy," he called, "they've come back as they said they would."

"Oh, lovely. And we've a goose for you, children. I hope you're hearty eaters."

"Some of us are," Tom said cheerfully.

They ate and talked and told the captain and his wife all that they had heard at Kendon's. It didn't seem to matter what they said, for the old couple knew the names and places and had a dozen stories for every one of theirs.

The travelers were sorry to have to leave, but they knew they had to use the midnight hours to get safely through the more settled mid-Cape fields and forests. With more thanks and blessings, they stood at the captain's door about to go.

Sara made a decision she'd been debating all evening. She took Ruth's small painting from her pack and offered it to Emmy. "It will remind you of the dunes."

"You can have my painting, Sara," Tom said as they

followed the path south in the darkness. "I like it, but you. . . ."

"Oh, Tom, that's . . . I don't know."

They made a brief detour that night at Tom's request. He wished to see the windmill at North Haven. This was a mid-eighteenth-century mill, which had been moved to its present location early in the eighteen hundreds and was at work grinding corn until the turn of the present century. It had been refurbished recently for the tourists.

The technology of the mill was simple and far older even than the Pilgrims' time, but another link somehow. It was a smock mill, with a hood, resembling a sailor's smock or poncho, that could be turned by hand to face the prevailing wind. A complex arrangement within, of iron gears and wooden shafts, drove a large grindstone at its base. Cornmeal was ground now on summer afternoons and bought in little bags by tourists. It was a thing of beauty and utility, as the settlers themselves had clearly known.

They roamed the mill's lofts and ladders and climbed the silent machinery to look out across the moonlit village green.

"Satisfactory?" Peter asked with just a hint of amusement.

"Highly," Tom said. He didn't elaborate, and they didn't ask. They found the path again and loped on into the night.

"I've decided," Tom said much later, as they trekked south toward their last day's camp before the marsh and

146

home, "to make a serious study of human history. I can run the wood shop and do that, too."

"Good lord," said Peter with a grin, "such a thing."

"We need to understand them, Peter, and there's a great deal to learn."

"I agree," Peter said more seriously, "and I'm very glad you want to do it. No one could do it better."

·20·

By the following night they were approaching familiar territory. The sea breeze carried just a hint of Cooper's Dump, a larger and less orderly affair than theirs. It lay directly in their path, and there seemed to them to be no reason to go all the way around it at this hour. The stench of smoldering trash grew stronger, and finally they saw the moonlit clearing through the trees. They paused a moment at its edge to marvel at the smoldering pits and tumbled remnants of a culture of unbridled waste.

"Awful," Sara volunteered.

"Awe inspiring," Tom amended.

"You're kidding?" Peter said.

"Sort of, but it's got to be all of a piece, doesn't it, dumps and farms and space travel?"

"Um," Peter said noncommittally. They crossed the barren dirt, swept clean daily by a now-silent power shovel. Embers crackled in the pits beside them. Nothing moved but their own dark shadows in the moonlight.

148

Suddenly the night came alive around them. A truck with only its parking lights burning surged from the entrance road, and then another and another, a half dozen huge construction trucks, and men on foot as well, directing them with flashlights. The rats' escape was blocked whichever way they turned.

"There," Peter cried. A pile of old stoves and refrigerators lay to one side of the main pit, waiting to be hauled to a salvage yard. They leaped inside an open refrigerator lying partly on its side.

"What the dickens—" Tom started to say.

"Illegal dumping. Toxic waste. What else could it be at midnight, with no lights?"

"Oh, great," Tom said, "and we're right in the middle of it."

"It's an opportunity for sociological research," Peter suggested dryly.

The trucks roared around them. Men shouted, and barrels tumbled into the dump. The big shovel was started and began to push dirt into the pits. It came steadily closer to the rats, and suddenly Sara saw it looming right above them.

"Jump," She shouted, and she leaped from the refrigerator just as the blade hit the pile. The refrigerator flipped and came to a stop face down, with Tom and Peter still inside, she realized.

Sara watched in horror as the shovel reversed and lined up to drive the entire pile into the dump, long before Tom and Peter could dig through the baked soil to freedom. What could she do, a two-pound rat, to stop a lumbering ten-ton machine? Not the machine, of course—the driver. She raced into the open and cleared one of the clanking tracks in a single great leap to land in the cab at the driver's feet. He never saw her, but he felt her teeth as she sank them into his calf. She remembered to let go just in time as the driver yelled and leaped to the ground. The power shovel lumbered on, directly toward Tom and Peter. The levers! She'd had just a glimpse of the man holding both controls. She grasped the right-hand lever with her jaws and hooked her rear claws into the fabric of the seat and pullled with all her will. The lever held; she lacked the strength. Shouts grew nearer. Would they try to stop it? They would see her. They would know. But it was that or abandon Tom and Peter to death. Then she felt the lever move, just slightly, and with a jerk the shovel turned abruptly in its course and headed for the pit. She jumped and was already in the shadow of the scrap pile when the big machine plunged over the edge, its engine roaring insanely. A flare shot out, and with a dull explosion the whole pit was filled with flames.

"Sara? Are you all right?" Peter's head appeared, where he had dug himself from beneath the refrigerator, his snout ludicrously encased in dirt.

"Me? I'm fine. Let's go. There's been a bit of a commotion."

Tom followed Peter from the hole, and the three of them raced for the opposite side of the clearing, now emptied of trucks and men. If anyone had seen them, they were too concerned with other matters to care.

They didn't stop until the noise and stench of the dump were far behind.

"Whoa," said Peter finally. "What commotion?"

Sara told them.

Tom just shook his head. "Thanks for our lives, Sara. That was pretty spectacular. What's happened to us, Peter? We seem to keep strolling to the edge of disaster. What kind of rats are we becoming?"

"Careless ones this time, I guess. It isn't enough just to stop acting like fools. We should have gone around. My fault."

"No, Peter. We're all big enough. We're just not paying attention to being rats, that's all. Let's decide not to be evolutionary rejects."

"Right," Peter agreed. "Thanks, Sara."

"I couldn't lose you, Peter—either of you."

"We do seem to need each other," Peter said.

They went on, more cautiously and talking softly in the dark.

"What about the dump?" Tom asked. "Illegal dumping here on the Cape?"

"They must have put the fire out pretty quickly," Sara said. "We didn't hear any sirens."

"Somebody has to notice the burned power shovel though," said Tom.

"Maybe," Peter said. "They'd have had to notice the barrels of waste, for that matter."

"You mean they already know about it?" Sara asked.

"Some of them must."

"Don't we have to tell someone?" Sara wasn't sure herself what she was saying, but she knew she felt offended and threatened by the dumpers. Surely something could be done.

"What about it, Peter?" Tom asked. "A letter to . . . the authorities?"

151

Peter didn't answer for a moment, as they moved rapidly along the now-familiar path. When he finally spoke, it was in an almost-unfamiliar voice.

"Write to someone if you feel you must, Tom. You, too, Sara. But I don't think we should interfere. We don't know enough, not yet. Once we start, where can it end? They won't work with us. They'd be out of their minds if they had the slightest suspicion theirs wasn't the only intelligence on this planet. Can you imagine? They'd wipe us out, and themselves in the process, probably. Maybe you can learn to understand them, Tom, and even find a way out for them, for all of us. And you can write about it, Sara, for the rats, so that we all might begin to realize our danger."

"I will," Sara said. "I'll write about this and about everything. I mean to be a writer." So that was settled now, no turning back.

"What are you going to do, Peter?" Tom asked. It was just a question.

"Learn calculus," Peter answered, with a chuckle, "and chemistry and biology. Figure out how life works. I've been thinking about what Ruth said on the beach. I've thought about it ever since. Her Tim has a talent that I don't have, but I can do some things very well; we all can. If Tim and Kendon can use their skills with all their might, so can we. And then we'll see." They walked on in silence.

"Who's there?" A small voice pierced the dark.

"John? Is that you?"

"Oh, Sara, you're back!" Her little brother came flying from the entrance to the den and nearly knocked her down.

"We're back and glad to be here," Sara said softly. "Let's go down, and we'll tell you all about it."

"Did anything neat happen?" John asked eagerly as they crossed the familiar stone porch.

"Oh, yes," Sara said. "A lot of good things happened."

"Up at North Cape?"

"Up there," she said, "and down here, too." Her weary thoughts took in the Cape and the marsh, Tom and Peter, and her own shadowy being as they plunged into the darkened entrance to the den. Their adventure had begun.